Today, I begin a new journey. A Journey to Caprice. A journey to a place I do not even know exists. We are all on this journey whether we know it or not. We might as well go together. Walk with me to Caprice. One Step at a Time.

Other Books by Rena Johnson

Answered Prayers Journal

Rena Johnson's Photography Workshop in a Book

Lake Sinclair in All Its Glory Photo Book

Co-Authored

God: An Amazing Artist and So Much More Photo Book

# Journey to Caprice

Caprice: Noun. 1. A sudden and unaccountable change of mood or behavior

## Rena Johnson

It All Started in a Garden

*To Sabrina,*
*I look forward to sharing the journey with you*
*Rena*

© 2024 Copyright Rena Johnson

All rights reserved. No part of this book may be reproduced in any form, written, verbal, electronically, or by artificial intelligence or transmitted in any form or by any means, without the prior written permission of the author, except where permitted by law.

ISBN: 979-8-218-40821-3

I would like to dedicate this book first to my wife Samantha Cooper for your unwavering support throughout this process. I could not have completed this novel as it is and at this time without you.

I would also like to thank my brother Larry Johnson and my sister Clearine Franks and my sister-in-law Shelia Johnson for all your support and encouragement throughout this entire process.

I would like to say a special thank you to Shelia Johnson for sharing one of her gorgeous paintings with me to use as the cover for the book. I knew the moment I saw it, that was somewhere I wanted to go. I hope all of you will agree after reading this book!

## A LIFE UNMANAGEABLE

Jessie was quite annoyed with herself as she pulled onto Paddington Way Drive. How did she allow herself to get talked into attending this re-reunion at such a dangerous time and all to celebrate a family she barely knew, even though it was the family she had unfortunately inherited?

She pulled her Wrangler into the first open spot she found. It just happened to be at the very back of the long driveway that led to her cousin's house. As she put the Jeep in park, she thought to herself, "At least parking back here it will not be as obvious when I make my early escape." Little did she know that leaving early, or maybe even at all, would prove to be far more difficult than she could ever begin to imagine.

She cut the car off and started to fumble around in it as though she was gathering her stuff together to bring to the party, even though her dish sat perfectly contained and ready to go on the seat next to her.

She put an empty drink bottle in her trash bag then gathered up some loose change and tossed it into the center console. She put some random mail into the glove box then lifted her sun visor. She adjusted her rearview mirror and at that moment she realized that she had completely run out of ways to procrastinate any further. So, with a heavy sigh, she opened the door, grabbed the dish from the passenger seat, checked her pocket for a mask in case she felt like she needed one, then stepped out of the jeep and uttered a half-hearted prayer. "Please let this be over sooner rather than later and don't let me do anything stupid or embarrassing." Then she closed the door, gave a quick glance up for emphasis and added "In Jesus' name."

She clicked her key fob to make sure the doors were locked, turned toward Cody's house, and started walking down the road that led to her destiny.

Each moment seemed to be moving in slow motion as she passed each of the other cars. Even as time was crawling at a snail's pace, her mind was racing. She expected the feelings of anxiety and the flood of memories being back with her family after all these years. What she did not expect was how out of sorts, even in her own skin, she would feel as this day's challenge began to get underway.

She decided to concentrate on her stroll down memory lane, hoping these other unidentifiable sensations would pass before she reached the end of the driveway.

She took notice of all the shiny, new, or at least exceptionally clean and well-kept vehicles, all perfectly parked as if in an upscale showroom of some sort. She suddenly wondered if she had parked straight at all. She was not really paying attention to how she parked. She sighed a bit of relief when she remembered that she had at least run her jeep through the car wash yesterday.

All these cars lined up in this way, somehow reminded her of going to church as a child and not too far from this very location. She still remembered how she felt all those many years ago.

The weekly event always seemed to start in the parking lot, the preparations for which always began the day before. She could remember clearly all those Saturday evenings spent with her parents and later grandparents preparing for church. Her dad, and later her granddad, always washed and waxed the outside of the "Family" car, while she cleaned the inside. Anytime there was any question about completing this ritual, the inarguable answer was always, "You never know who we might need to give a ride to or from church tomorrow." It was always said with such certainty and commitment as if it were the one thing, they were commissioned to do by God Himself. Questioning it might as well have been questioning the entire existence of the thread that held it all together.

Jessie often wondered exactly who in church would rank high enough in their opinion to elicit that ongoing activity week after week, month after month, year after year throughout most of Jessie's childhood. This curiosity was enhanced even more because Jessie could count on one hand the number of times they had ever actually given a ride to anyone at all.

There were a lot of things they did to prepare for "Church on Sunday" that did not really make a lot of sense to her back then, and still did not to some degree. But we will get to more of those things later.

Jessie had reached the end of the car exhibit and was now entering the perfectly manicured lawn. As she glanced ahead, she could see Cody's new house in the distance. She was looking forward to seeing her house and her. "Maybe the party won't be that bad if I don't panic and can stay clear of the majority of the people." As an afterthought she said to herself, "And if I can somehow shake this feeling that the whole world is about to turn upside down." She shook her head and took her first step into the yard.

Walking alone down the driveway, she thought it might be easy not to draw attention to herself, but now that task became impossible. Even though the well-kept yard appeared to have its own garden staff assigned to it, there were freshly fallen, crisp leaves all over the place and more were constantly joining them in the fresh breeze. Autumn was certainly on full display here. Every single step she took seemed to elicit a crunch that exploded inside her brain.

Normally she loved this time of year, but not when every 3 or 4 seconds, it caused someone else to turn and look at her. Each gaze seemed different from the last. Some of these strangers smiled at her and then quickly, almost too quickly, turned their attention back to the current speaker in their group. Others looked at her quizzically as though maybe she was lost and had found herself in the wrong place altogether. Still others seemed to be purposefully ignoring her completely.

A dozen or so small children ran across the yard ahead of her. They were playing their very own version of soccer, where the goal of the game seemed to be simply keeping the ball away from all the other kids for the longest amount of time possible. Watching these kids having so much fun lowered her anxiety for a moment but that was very short lived.

Suddenly, their bright red and white ball came bouncing in Jessie's direction. She felt a rush of anxiety rising inside of her, as much to her dismay, the ball came straight to her. It bumped awkwardly into her foot and slowly rolled to a stop a couple of feet away from her. Jessie looked up at the expectant kids. She knew she had to do something. She took a step toward the ball and nervously kicked it back toward them. It seemed to Jessie as if all eyes, young, old, and everywhere in between, were suddenly staring her down. Time once again moved in slow motion as the ball half-heartedly rolled to a stop three or four feet shy of where the closest kid was standing.

"Thanks Lady," one of the kids yelled. Jessie gave the kids a thumbs up, then looked around and saw that at least a dozen or so parents were indeed watching her. She smiled and shrugged her shoulders as if to say, "That is why I never pursued any sports in school or otherwise." At least that is what she hoped it conveyed. Jessie forcibly looked ahead and continued to make her way toward the gorgeous house that awaited before her.

She finally reached the bottom of the stairs leading up to the wraparound porch. She took a deep breath and started up the beautiful, wide entranceway that gave an air of historical preservation to this otherwise new looking home. She carefully watched each step she took so as not to trip and make an even bigger fool of herself than she felt she did with the ball. She also politely navigated around the few people standing or sitting along the way to avoid any unnecessary interactions with them.

She reached the top of the stairs without incident and quickly crossed the porch. When she reached the door, she paused only for a brief second as she uttered again to herself, "God help me." Then she turned the doorknob and went inside.

Immediately she found herself in a room full of people of whom she did not recognize a single one. She suddenly felt a rush of inner panic and wondered to herself if maybe she had accidentally gone to the wrong house for real. "At least some of these people should look somewhat familiar," she pointed out to herself. She looked around trying to decide where to go from here.

As a small group of older ladies closest to her turned and looked at her, she held up her dish, almost as a sort of peace offering or more honestly, as a shield.

One of the ladies smiled cautiously and headed her way. Jessie was quite sure by the look on her face that she did not recognize her either. At least they were on mutual ground there. "Follow me dear, and I will show you where the dining room is."

Jessie followed this woman down the hall and into the dining room. "What did you bring, dear?"

"Squash casserole."

"Oh, I love squash casserole. Let's clear out a spot here for it with the other casseroles."

"Perfect." Jessie took the dish out of the warmer bag, laid the bag flat on the counter and set her casserole on top of it, as it seemed everyone else had done before her. "Thank you."

"Sure thing, dear. Grab a cup there at the end of the counter and pour yourself a glass of homemade lemonade. It is rather good if I do say so myself." She winked at Jessie and headed back down the hall to her friends. Jessie was surprised that the woman did not ask her more questions about who she was but felt relieved at the same time.

Jessie suddenly found herself alone in this huge, beautiful dining room full of every kind of food imaginable. Every counterspace was covered. She was not sure what to do next but getting lemonade would at least give her something to do with her hands.

They trembled a bit as she poured her drink. She decided not to fill her glass all the way to the top just in case the trembling got worse.

Just as she was putting the jug back on the counter, she heard a familiar voice.

"Jessie! You made it!"

She turned around to see her cousin Cody smiling as she headed her way with arms stretched out.

"Hey Cuz! "How are you doing?" Jessie said, genuinely smiling and feeling a huge sense of relief as she reached out to embrace Cody.

"I am great! Running around like crazy of course, but you know I love this sort of thing. I am so glad you made it."

"Well, of course. I promised you I would come. I have never stood you up before, have I, at least without calling first?" she joked as she smiled at Cody.

"Yay. I am so glad. So, what do you think of my new digs?" Cody looked around the dining room as if trying to see it through Jessie's eyes.

"Oh, it is gorgeous, absolutely gorgeous and so big."

"Yes, I got such a great deal on this place. There is so much I want to do with it but for now, I just want to get through this party and take the rest of the week off. Are you going to stick around for a couple of days?" Cody looked at her with a bit of a pout. Then joked, "You could help clean up after the party?" They both chuckled.

"As enticing as that sounds, I will probably head back home right after dinner. I have work tomorrow."

"Oh, that sucks. Well then, I hate your job right now more than you do!"

"I do not hate it, I just ... "Jessie paused because she really was at a loss as to how she feels about her job and did not want to get into a long discussion about it, at least not here today.

"I know you don't hate it. It is a wonderful job, and you make a lot more of a positive impact there than you think you do, but I know you could do so much more. However, selfishly, I just want to spend more time with you."

"Awe, we will. Now that I know where your new house is, I will visit again soon, well as soon as you are all settled into it."

"You are always welcome, settled or not" Cody said as she smiled genuinely at Jessie.

Jessie smiled back noticing how beautiful Cody looked, especially with the sunshine coming in through the window lighting up her long sandy brown, curly hair. Cody was another one of those perfect family members, but she always made Jessie feel totally accepted. "I will come back soon. I promise."

"Okay Jessie, I will hold you to that. But for now, come say hello to everyone. "

Jessie felt her smile fade as her heartbeat sped up and dread began to fill her entire being once again.

"Oh, don't be like that. Come on, you are going to enjoy yourself." She reassured Jessie as if intuitively reading every word of her body language.

Jessie knew the time had come and socialize she must.

The next few minutes became a frenzy of "hellos" followed almost exclusively by "how are you?" stated in such a way as to convey Jessie was some long lost relative, they were all so excited to see. Jessie was sure they were just as clueless about who she was as she was about them. Jessie started to feel a bit overwhelmed and even a bit dizzy at one point, but at least the time was ticking by. She was making her appearance and would hopefully be able to slip away right after dinner.

The excitement seemed to die down a little bit in her direction as a new family appeared at the front door. Jessie took this opportunity to step back from the crowd a bit.

At the same time, Cody excused herself from the group to go finish getting dinner ready.

"Can I help?" Jessie asked, hoping for an excuse to busy herself with anything other than trying to talk to any more of these other people she did not really know.

"Nope, I got it. Mingle. Mingle." Cody said as she winked at Jessie and disappeared around the corner.

Mingle was the last thing that Jessie wanted to do. Since all the strangers in this immediate group were now distracted, especially with the newly appeared family's baby, Jessie took her chance and slipped away back down the hallway.

She found her way back to the dining room and poured herself another cup of lemonade, still being careful not to fill it all the way full. She expected to see Cody any minute but then heard her talking with someone in the next room. So, she took a long drink of the lemonade and allowed the taste to fill her very being. It really was exceptionally good, even by Jessie's strict lemonade standards. Although, at this point, it might have been more helpful if it were a bit harder, she thought to herself, but she knew that the un-doctored version was most certainly her better choice in such a situation.

She picked up the pitcher again and topped it off one more time. Then readying herself to walk down the hall again toward the front room, she silently muttered another prayer under her breath for God to help her get through this as quickly and unscathed as possible. Had she known what was coming, she would have realized that sometimes our plans and God's are not the same.

Just as she started to head toward the hall, the lady that initially brought her to the dining room was back and seemed quite happy to see Jessie with more lemonade. Jessie told her how good it was. Then for reasons unknown, she asked the lady for directions to the bathroom. She really did not need to go, but she supposed that would take up a few more minutes and cut off any additional conversation this woman might want to have. The lady smiled, pointed down the hall and said, "Last door on the right." Then the lady turned and went down the hall the other way.

Jessie headed down the hall slowly. She stopped to look at all the different pictures hanging on the wall as she went. She had seen at least half of these images in Cody's old house but decided to take the time to look at them closer now. She was happy doing anything that would take a bit more time and did not involve mingling. While looking at these images, she felt her anxiety start to wane a bit, completely unaware of what waited for her only five or six steps away.

She saw images of kids playing sports, other portraits that looked like senior pics, over a dozen group shots of Cody and her friends in various places around the world as well as another dozen or so beautiful landscape scenes. Cody was well known for her incredible people photography and was always flying off to one destination or another for a new shoot or client.

Then Jessie stopped in front of the biggest picture of them all right in the middle of the hallway.

Ah, it was the group shot from the last family reunion the summer before the pandemic. Jessie looked at each of the smiling faces and remembered seeing only about half of them but could name far fewer. She had already seen ten or so of the same unknown faces here today. There were at least a couple people from this image that she knew would not be here as they had died from the virus in the last few years. Thinking about that made her notice how carefree they all looked back then. Everyone at the party today pretty much looked the same way now, but Jessie knew better. Nothing was the same. No one was the same. The world was not the same, nor would it ever truly be. Yet, as surreal as it seemed, here she was herself, smiling and trying to function as if everything was okay.

As she scanned the reunion image, she saw herself on the far-right hand side of it. She looked as out of place then as she was feeling today. While everyone else in the image seemed genuinely happy, all dressed up with every hair in place, Jessie looked like she did not even belong to the same family. She wore a pullover hoodie, blue jeans, a fake smile, and her hair looked like a windblown mess.

As she looked closer, she realized there was even a noticeable stain on the sweatshirt she had been wearing. She thought to herself how odd that was because she still had that sweatshirt and knew that it did not have a stain like that on it. It is one of her favorites and most comfortable shirts she owns. She still wears it all the time but there is no spot like that on it even now and never had been as far as she knew. "So, why was it there then, so clear in this image?" she wondered to herself.

As she looked closer trying to figure out what that stain might have been, everything seemed to get a little blurry for a moment. She blinked her eyes a couple of times, looked away and then looked back. Suddenly she noticed that everything else in the image seemed in perfect focus, except her, and especially that stain on her sweatshirt.

Jessie decided to focus harder and see if she could tell what the spot was. She leaned in to get an even closer look and suddenly felt as though the spot grew a tiny bit larger. She quickly backed up, shook her head, and looked away then back at it again. "That's odd." She thought to herself.

It was not like Cody to get part of an image out of focus or leave something like that in one of her pictures. She is quite meticulous about her photography. That is part of why she is so successful in her career. Yet, here was this whole area on this one that was very much out of focus and very obviously a stain that should not have been there. "Why wouldn't Cody have just taken that out of the image altogether?" she wondered to herself. "I have seen her do stuff like that before." She sighed and let out a quiet, "curious, very curious."

Jessie blinked again and tried to look even closer at the spot. This time it appeared that the very molecules that made up the canvas itself were starting to move around a little bit. Nervously she closed her eyes tight for a moment and then tried to see the whole image better. The rest of the image seemed okay. She glanced back at the spot one more time trying not to go into panic mode.

This time it was noticeably larger than before and seemed to be swirling around in a semi-circle sort of pattern.

Startled and a bit unnerved by this whole thing, Jessie decided to just walk away and forget this ever happened. "Maybe I just need some food." She justified this to herself by recalling that she had only eaten a cup of applesauce earlier today. In fact, she did feel quite hungry. "That must be it."

Hopefully, it was almost time to eat, and all of this would just be a weird little thing that she would never tell anyone about. Little did she know, her little secret was about to get much more intense.

She decided to continue to the bathroom, wash her face and walk back to the dining area. Even if they were not all eating yet, she could grab a bite of something, and it would surely help her feel better.

In the bathroom, Jessie washed her face and dried it on a paper towel. There were several towels hanging in the bathroom, but she was not sure which one to use, so the paper towel seemed less awkward. She looked at herself in the mirror and wondered why she always fretted about such trivial things.

To the right of the mirror, Jessie saw a cute picture of a little girl walking on the beach. She thought she would examine that image more closely and see if she had the same sort of experience as before. There was a seashell in the foreground of the image, so she got close and stared at it for a moment, but nothing happened. No movement, no swirls, nothing.

"Hmm." she thought to herself. "Maybe there was some weird lighting in the hall that she hadn't noticed." That thought along with a lack of swirling seashells made her feel a little better.

Whatever it was that made her feel as though the image was moving in front of her eyes seemed to have stopped. So, Jessie sighed in relief, left the bathroom, and headed back down the hall.

She decided to not even look at the image from last year's family reunion as she walked by it, purposefully looking at the images on the other side of the hall. She almost made it. However, a bit of movement in the corner of her eye caught her attention and with a total lack of self-control, she glanced over at the image.

Sure enough, the spot she saw before was, without a doubt, still moving and it had now doubled in size.

She could see it swirling from halfway across the hall now. Jessie felt a queasiness in her stomach, her eyes started to water, and she could feel her hands, in fact, her entire body, begin to shake nervously. Her thoughts started racing as she felt a sense of panic coming over her.

She closed her eyes and tried to focus on the sounds of the party around her. She could hear laughter and people talking in other rooms just down the hall. She heard piano music farther away in the house. Outside the nearest window, there was someone listening to sports scores, and she thought she could smell cigarette smoke. As she took this all in, she felt slightly less alone. She also felt a mild sense of camaraderie with the person outside the window. Even though she would never be interested herself in either of those things, it was nice to know she was not the only person at the party that would rather be somewhere else.

Feeling slightly less panicked, she turned her head away from the image, opened her eyes and tried to force herself to start walking down the hall again and completely ignore the picture on the wall, especially the swirling figment of her imagination part of it.

"It has to be a blood sugar issue or something" she told herself again. "I just need to let it go, walk to the dining room, grab a cookie or something, and it will all go away."

Suddenly annoyed and feeling unsteady, she purposefully regained her balance and added silently to herself, "As if just having to be here was not hard enough, now I have to deal with all this weirdness on top of it. Come on God, help me out here."

Before she could even take the first step down the hall, her feeling of annoyance began to morph into something else. She now felt a whole different kind of emotion overtaking her. She hated her life sometimes. It was so out of control, and nothing ever seemed to work out the way she wanted it to. She had promised herself again last year, like she did every year on her birthday, which was only a few days away, that everything would be so much different by this time this year. Yet here she was, with another year of her life gone. She was still in the same dead-end job, barely making enough money to get by. She was not effecting any positive change in the world like she had hoped. She was still lonely with only a couple of house plants to keep her company. She often felt as though she was barely even keeping them alive. At times like this, it seemed like a bout of serious depression might be knocking at her door, except it was always overshadowed by this annoying little itch deep inside her spirit that told her there was so much more to life that was just barely beyond her current grasp. In fact, the latter feeling was an almost constant companion at times, but she felt so hopeless to do anything about it.

Catching herself just before falling down the figurative rabbit hole, she took a deliberate step toward the dining room and away from this negative space she was creating. As she did, she whispered to herself, "God help me turn my life around please. I know the entire world is a mess right now. Believe me, I know you have your hands full, but I really need to turn my little piece of it around. Please help me make sense of it all and understand what these feelings I have are." As she muttered this almost subconscious prayer, without even realizing it, she turned her eyes back toward the image.

She felt another surge of panic course through her veins as she saw the swirling vortex of her pre-diabetes now growing larger by the second. Suddenly, she had an idea. If she reached out and physically touched the image, surely that would dispel this illusion and she would be able to let it go and walk away.

She started to reach out toward the canvas but felt a sudden rush of fear. "What if touching it had the opposite effect?" she wondered. She paused then leaned in to get an even closer look at it. "Could it be some sort of electrical current or shortage just behind the picture that was about to set the canvas on fire or something like that?" She had never seen or even heard of anything like that before, but she had not ever seen anything like this before either. At this point, knowing what was going on was worth the risk of getting shocked. But she still leaned in for a closer look before touching it.

As she got closer, she could see thousands of little particles swirling together, as if the atmosphere itself was slowly dissolving the image. Beginning to panic again and feeling as if she had no other choice than to touch it and try to shatter the illusion, she slowly reached out her hand. Using only her index finger, she very cautiously touched the swirl.

It was a weird sensation. It did not feel like a canvas print at all. It did not even feel solid. But it did not feel like liquid or any other substance she had ever felt before either. It felt more like energy or something, but thankfully not an electrical current. Even though she would have almost welcomed a slight shock or something that would give indication of a semi-rational reason for it, she had no such luck. Instead of a shock, she felt something more like a cool breeze, as if she had opened a cooler of ice on a hot, summer day. Instead of an electrical jolt, she felt a sense of refreshment begin to wash over her as the cool air encompassed her finger and seemed to, ever so slightly, engulf her entire hand.

With her touch, the swirl began to expand again very slowly. It was large enough now that Jessie felt the cool breeze on her entire arm. Instinctively, she leaned forward, knowing the cool breeze would feel good on her flushed face. She was not usually hot natured and would tend to get cold before others around her, but suddenly this hallway seemed overly warm to her. She told herself that at least feeling hot made sense with all the cooking going on just down the hall in the kitchen and every room filled with people.

As she drew a little closer, the cool air on her face felt amazing. She took a deep breath and could swear she now smelled her favorite scent, wild honeysuckle.

The next thought that came to her was that maybe she was having some sort of physical altercation within herself. Maybe a stroke? Or an aneurism? Or maybe she had a brain tumor, and this is how it was presenting itself? Or maybe someone had just spiked the lemonade. "Was it all a hallucination?" She had never had one before, but that could certainly explain the majority of this, if not all.

Whatever was happening felt completely out of her control and, at least for the moment, she was surrounded by a welcoming cool breeze and the most wonderful smell on earth. She decided to just enjoy the moment, especially since she felt completely powerless to do anything about it anyway.

Slowly she realized the anchors to the real world were beginning to fade away. The sports scores she heard through the window were slowly replaced by the sounds of birds singing. Had they turned off their game and came back inside and the birds started singing in their place or was something else happening?

Jessie began to focus on those beautiful songs and tried to imagine what kind of birds were making those lovely sounds. As the volume of the singing rose, all the chatter and other noises going on in the house around her faded.

Without even realizing it, Jessie had closed her eyes as she thought to herself how nice this little break turned out to be. She had gone to the bathroom just to waste five or so minutes and then had this little reprieve along the way. "Okay God, this is not horribly bad."

She suddenly became aware of the fact that she was standing in the hall of her cousin's house in the middle of a huge party with her eyes closed with her hand stretched out touching a random image. If any of her family came down the hall, they would absolutely think she had completely lost her mind. She quickly opened her eyes and looked around. Thankfully, no one was there. The hall now seemed unbearably hot, humid, noisy, and as if the very air itself was stale but heavy with overpowering scents.

A circus of food smells wafted down the hall from the kitchen along with the faint smell of recently cut grass that must have been coming in through the window now that the smell of smoke had dissipated.

She could hear a dozen or so people talking but it sounded like a jumbled-up mess. She could not make out what any one person was saying. Not that she really cared anyway.

After one more quick check down the hall in both directions, she slowly turned her attention back to the image and the swirling vortex before her. Almost at once, she felt the cool breeze again, heard the birds singing and smelled the honeysuckle, all of which filled her entire being with a feeling of such contentment and relaxation it put her soul at ease.

Jessie concluded it was not a medical emergency like an aneurism or anything like that, since it all went away when she forced herself to look up and down the hall, but the illusion was right there as soon as she chose to look back at the picture. That realization brought with it a sense of relief as well as an overwhelming feeling of curiosity.

Once again, she leaned toward the image. This time, as soon as she started to get close to it, she could feel a breeze gently blowing her hair and felt the sense of peace begin to engulf the whole top part of her body, as well as all her other senses.

She slowly took a deep breath enjoying the honeysuckle and realizing that the cut grass smell was coming to her from this illusion rather than through the bathroom window. Closing her eyes, she began to let out a peaceful sigh and her world began to change.

## COMING TO BELIEVE

Suddenly she felt as though she was floating. She opened her eyes but could not see anything at all. She quickly put out both hands for balance and to brace herself just in case she was in fact falling.

It was a weird sensation; unlike anything she had ever felt before. She was quite sure she had just become unconscious for some reason or possibly even died.

She felt as if she were in some sort of suspended animation, floating but not quite moving, but still sure, maybe even hoping, that she was about to hit the wall or floor.

The floating sensation increased. All senses of the physical world or any sort of balance or direction were gone. Again, she felt a bout of panic begin to overtake her. She tried to regain control of her thoughts as well as her body.

She felt as though at any moment she would start spinning out of control and into oblivion or worse. She tried desperately to straighten herself back upright, even though at this point, she was not even sure which direction was up.

Just as she was about to go into full panic mode, she felt her feet slowly touching the ground and her sense of balance returning. Unfortunately, she still could not see anything. She blinked a couple more times, then closed her eyes for a moment before reopening them. Still nothing.

As her feet became more firmly planted on the ground, it felt as though she was standing barefoot on a thick carpet of cool grass, rather than the hardwood floors of the hallway. She did not dare to move in case she fell over or lost all sense of herself again.

She decided to concentrate on the ground under her feet, and just be present and calm as she tried to become aware of her surroundings. The cool breeze she had felt moments ago slowly came back but was now all around her. She noticed it was the perfect temperature, not too hot or cold. It was perfect, which was not a common feeling for her, especially over the last couple of years.

Jessie lowered her arms down by her side and took a couple of deep breaths with her eyes closed. She slowly opened them. Even as she willed them with all her might to see whatever was around her, she still could not see anything. It was very disconcerting. She quickly closed her eyes again.

Her ears had no trouble at all adjusting to this new state of being. The sounds of birds were all around her and she could hear water running in the distance like the trickle of a mountain stream.

As she concentrated on all those sounds, her eyes felt as though they were very slowly opening without any effort on her part. As her eye lids slowly rose, she could see light and color all around her, but no forms whatsoever. It was as if she were looking very closely at a beautiful abstract painting. However, it was all very disorienting, so she purposefully closed her eyes, took another deep breath, and opened them again.

This time she could just barely make out a beautiful meadow stretching out before her. It was as if she was looking at a living, breathing, abstract work of art from within it. Slowly something at the end of the meadow started to appear as well, but she could not make out what it was.

She closed her eyes tightly again and then slowly opened them. The grass of the field came into even clearer focus now as did the beautiful blue waters of a lake just beyond the meadow. Slowly, everything around her came into focus. She was in the most beautiful place she could have ever imagined.

The meadow was filled with the most magnificent flowers of all colors and sizes. She took a deep breath again, this time keeping her eyes open. It was as if her very essence was being caressed with the wonderful smell of flowers and grass, even by the fresh air surrounding her. She had never felt as peaceful as she did at this moment in time.

The lake shimmered in the distance, reflecting the most pristine blue sky with fluffy white clouds and now she could see it was framed by magnificent snowcapped mountains in the background. She had never seen any place like this before, at least not in person. "Where in the world am I?" she asked aloud but was quite happy no one was there to answer her.

She was now certain that at least a part of her was no longer still standing in Cody's hallway in front of that picture. "Does this mean I do have a tumor or an aneurism or something? Maybe I am now in a coma or have even died? From the looks of this place, maybe I have even gone to heaven already."

As these thoughts were running through her head, she started to feel quite out of sorts again. Her mind raced back to the reunion. Was she still standing there in the hall but having a hallucination? Maybe there was something in that lemonade she was allergic to or could the woman that made it be into some crazy stuff no one else suspected. In today's world, you just never know.

Her family might be gathered around her right now. If so, were they whispering to each other about how they had always suspected her of being crazy and now she had proven it. That thought made her feel far more anxious than thinking she might be dead. She felt herself wishing for the latter. At least then she would not have to deal with all the stress of her life anymore. She felt her heart begin to race and knew she needed to calm down.

Once again, she closed her eyes and with determination to distinguish reality from hallucination, she slowly opened them again.

Suddenly everything was clear in her entire line of vision. This place was teaming with life, the flowers blowing in the breeze, a variety of birds were flying over the lake and one large fish after another jumped right in the middle of it. She could hear the splashes even from here and see the ripples in the water flow out in all directions. Those waves turned the lake into a sort of kaleidoscope reflecting all the colors of the rainbow in one beautiful circle after another.

Without even thinking about it, she tried to take a step toward the lake. Suddenly it felt as though she was losing her balance again and maybe even falling. She closed her eyes and tried to steady herself. She opened her eyes again slowly and looked around. Everything looked even more solid. She also felt solid enough herself but moving seemed currently beyond her ability.

Whatever brought her here, she at least wanted to be able to explore this beautiful place. If she was stuck here and not able to explore it at all, maybe this was her own personal hell. With that thought she knew she had to try again.

She stretched out both arms to brace herself in case she fell then willed herself to take a step forward. This time she very awkwardly felt her right foot move forward and haphazardly touch back down in the cool grass. She cautiously began to shift her weight to that foot in preparation for taking another step.

The next step seemed a fraction of a bit easier. Now with both feet firmly underneath her and knowing she had taken a full step forward, she decided to keep moving.

She put her hands in front of her again just in case she ran into the now invisible wall in the hall. But her hands found nothing solid. She completed the next step, far more easily. So, she tried another one. Each step was a little easier than the one before.

She was headed in the direction of the lake but had no idea how close or far away it was. Every step she took seemed to bring her closer to the lake than it should have. Each step also felt as though she was somehow floating yet perfectly connected to the ground at the same time. There was a feeling in this place as if everything were somehow connected by some higher energy or power that was yet unseen.

Jessie laughed to herself and thought, "Maybe this really is heaven or paradise or something, because floating along like this, I feel like I have finally lost those extra few pounds I have tried to lose for so long."

At that moment she decided to look down at herself. "Whoa, where is my body?" She could almost see it but not quite. It was as if she could see the energy or aura of her body, but not the physical body itself. At least that explained why she felt so light.

After a moment of trying to just be present and accept this illusion of not having an actual physical presence here, she took another deep breath. This time she did not want to close her eyes for fear it would all vanish, and she would be back in that hallway again or worse. She took another step.

As Jessie continued her journey toward the lake, her mind was both simultaneously at peace and flooded with the same questions. "What is this place? Am I dead? Am I hallucinating? Is this heaven? How did I get here? Why am I here?"

Jessie replied to her own questions racing through her mind, "I do not know how I got here, but I love it better than any place I have ever been, so if it took dying or worse, like losing my mind, to get here, so be it. I hope it lasts as long as possible. I would love to stay right here forever."

Just as she was about to thank God for allowing her to find such an incredible paradise and have it all to herself, she started to hear random different but faint noises. She thought she could almost hear sounds of someone talking or children laughing in the far distance.

She was disheartened to think she must be coming out of this episode, coma, or whatever it was. These must be sounds from the reunion somehow finding its way into this reality. She did not want to wake up. She tried to concentrate on the sights before her and the sounds of the birds in the air and breeze in the trees rather than the sounds she thought were coming from the party.

She purposefully continued toward the lake. However, as she drew closer to it, she could hear the laughter even louder. She purposefully blinked her eyes a couple of times to try to see if that might bring anyone else into focus. She was not sure she wanted to know where those sounds were coming from, but she felt like she needed to figure it out. But even after two or three more attempts at some sort of ocular restart, she still could not see anyone, anywhere in this place. Yet, the sounds were still there and getting louder.

About halfway to the lake, she decided to turn around and see where she had just come from.

She half expected to see a huge black hole or some sort of vortex swirling right there behind where she had been standing. But there was nothing of the sort. There was just the other half of the field full of flowers and a wooded forest area, gently cradling the meadow where she was currently standing. It was amazingly beautiful but quite disconcerting.

Looking back toward the lake, she was sure she could hear people talking now. The sounds were very faint, and she could not make out a single word they were saying, but they were, without a doubt, people's voices.

As disheartened as she felt about this, she again looked all around to see if she could see anyone. She could see clearly for a long distance in every direction and there was absolutely no one in sight. "It has to be voices wafting over from the party," she thought to herself.

She turned and headed back down toward the lake. She wanted to enjoy every minute she had left here, whether it was a minute, a month or forever.

Just as she started to move toward the lake again, she could have sworn she saw movement out of the corner of her eye. She looked around but saw nothing. The leaves were blowing ever so slightly through the trees just beyond the meadow. "It must have been that or a bird flying over, or a bug flying by or something like that." she tried to convince herself.

She continued her journey toward the lake. At least walking had become easier, and she no longer felt like she was going to lose her balance with each step she took.

It was such a beautiful autumn day here and the sky was SO blue reflecting onto the lake below. It looked like a scene straight out of a dream, except she knew she was not asleep when all this started, so it had to be something else entirely. Knowing that, however, did not diminish the beauty of it in the least.

The almost surreal color on the trees made it all still look like a painting. Autumns back in the real world were never quite this beautiful. You might see a little color here or there, but there always seemed to be more brown leaves than colored ones, at least in her experience and in the area where she lived. Jessie loved autumn but always felt disappointed in it for that very reason. Everyone always talked about the amazing color season that was coming and had such high hopes of a stunning display only to have those hopes destroyed day by day as the leaves mostly just turned brown and fell off. Then of course, that letdown was followed by miserable cold, rain, snow, and ice for the next several months. Yeah, Autumn had never been what it was geared up to be. But here, it was quite spectacular.

As she stared at the leaves on the trees for a moment longer, she began to feel a true sense of appreciation for nature, even beyond what she had always felt before.

Then movement once again caught her attention. She quickly looked down across the meadow to the edge of the woods and just watched there for three or four minutes or so it seemed. She saw the movement again. Then suddenly, out of the edge of the woods, walked a big, beautiful white tail buck with a huge rack of antlers. She had never seen anything like it in person before. As Jessie watched, he casually and majestically walked out into the sunlight. Then he began walking around the edge of the woods while snacking on the greenest grass imaginable right in the same meadow where she stood. He did not seem to pay any attention to her whatsoever.

Jessie watched him and could barely control her excitement. He finally looked up at her as well, but with far less excitement. Then more movement caught her attention. A couple more deer strolled out of the woods down where he had appeared from moments ago.

Then Jessie heard another huge fish jump in the lake and looked around to see the ripples slowly fan out across the lake. She glanced back toward where the deer were and saw a couple more coming out of the woods. These looked much smaller. They did not have spots like newborn fawns but were obviously still young or of a different breed or something.

As she stood there gazing out across the field, watching the deer, listening to the sounds of birds, as well as crickets and other insects as they all sang in perfect harmony, she started seeing more movements in all directions. There were all kinds of birds visible now flying overhead, as well as a couple of rabbits hopping about here and there in the grass so peacefully, just thoroughly enjoying their day. Then suddenly off to the left of the field appeared a fox. "This could be bad news for the rabbits," Jessie thought. Thankfully though, the fox seemed perfectly content to sit in the sun and bath himself, paying the rabbits no attention whatsoever.

Jessie turned her attention back to the lake. She really wanted to get closer to it. Even with the blue sky reflecting on it, Jessie could tell it looked perfectly clear. She wanted to see for herself just how clear it was. As soon as she made the decision to walk farther down there, she felt herself drawing nearer to it. She reached the water's edge with only minimal effort on her part.

She looked down and sure enough, the water was so clear she could see beautiful pebbles covering the bottom of the lake as well as fish swimming all around in it. She had never seen water so clear before.

Overcome with sheer joy, she decided to sit down on a nearby rock and just enjoy the view for a while. She would love to sit down on that lush green grass. However, she was sure there would be a million bugs in it plus she was somewhat allergic to grass, so the rock was a better choice. As suddenly as she made that decision, she found herself sitting there.

She had only been sitting there a couple of minutes when she started to hear the voices again. They were still very faint but seemed to be growing a bit louder. She was sure she could also hear children laughing in the distance. She looked around in every direction and tried to see where those sounds were coming from. But there was no one anywhere in sight. Again, Jessie hoped she was not starting to wake up from this amazing, well, whatever it was. She loved being here in her own personal paradise and really wished she could stay here forever.

She had never felt so at peace in every way. She felt absolutely zero stress, worry, or even pain of any sort, which was a bit odd for her. With her auto immune disorder always wreaking havoc with her body, there was always something aching somewhere.

She decided to take advantage of every minute, every second and try to ignore the voices for as long as she could. Maybe they would just go away.

But instead, they seemed to grow slightly louder with every passing minute.

Jessie whispered "God, please let me stay here, at least a little longer."

Then almost at once she heard someone say her name.

"Hi Jessie." This was followed quickly by,

"We are so glad you are here."

## ALLION

"What?" Jessie called out. "Who is there?"

"Thank you for coming to visit us here."

"Who said that?' Now Jessie was starting to feel a sense of panic. Why could she hear voices but not see anyone? Everything else here seemed as real and solid as anything she had ever known, but obviously there was something more going on with these voices. Apparently, she was still back in that hall at her family's house because there certainly did not seem to be anybody else present in whatever this place was, not that she could see in front of her anyway. Although, come to think of it, even if she were back at Cody's house, who was talking to her in this way and why could they see her, but she could not see them? What was happening? She questioned which one was real, what she could see or what she could hear? As Jessie's panic level rose, she heard one of the voices again, this time it was clearer and closer sounding.

"Just relax Jessie. It is all okay. We are just so glad you are here."

"How can I relax when I am hearing voices and don't know where I am or who is talking to me? Am I dead? What is happening? Instead of relaxing, her stress level was rising quickly.

A very calm voice answered her, "No Jessie, you are not dead. You are perfectly safe and very much alive."

"So, am I hallucinating? I do not understand what is happening here."

"No Jessie, everything you see is perfectly real."

"It is all too perfect to be real and if it is real, why can't I see you?"

"You will see us when you are ready."

"Us? What do you mean? How many of you are there? I am ready. I do want to see who is talking to me!" Jessie tried to convince whoever was talking to her to show themselves, which in all honesty, she was not sure at all if she was ready to know what was truly happening.

"Jessie, just relax. Enjoy the view. Know that you are safe and just be present in the moment.

Soon enough all your questions will be answered."

Jessie took a deep breath, closed her eyes then slowly opened them again as she let out a long sigh trying to slow her panic.

Everything was still as it was before, except there seemed to be more distortions here and there. It reminded Jessie of how heat looks when it rises from hot pavement.

She took another deep breath and tried intently to see those distortions clearer somehow. But the harder she tried the less she could see them. Her heart raced as she tried to figure out if these disruptions in her vision were the source of those voices. Once again, she closed her eyes and tried to calm down. When she opened her eyes, the distortions were back, but still not clear.

"It is okay Jessie. Just know that we are not going to hurt you. Just take your time and enjoy your surroundings. We have waited a long time to show you this place."

Even though Jessie could still not make out where the voices were coming from, she decided to ask them questions anyway. "What is this place?"

"Welcome to Caprice, Jessie. Again, we are so glad you came to visit us here."

"What or where is Caprice? I have never heard of it. Is it part of the afterlife? Am I dreaming or hallucinating? What is going on? Please tell me something. I am freaking out here!"

"Caprice is none of those things. Caprice is a real place. It is also a state of being. A state of awareness. It is peace realized. In the world you are used to, the word Caprice is a noun and means a sudden and unaccountable change of mood or behavior. Here, it simply means to truly live in the moment of life itself, and in a way that is truly sustaining and for the overall greater good and doing so intentionally."

"It certainly is changing my mood to be here. It also happened suddenly, and all of this is certainly unaccounted for, so at least the name makes sense, even if absolutely nothing else does." Jessie almost laughed aloud when she said that. For something, anything, in this world to make sense or even in her own world for that matter, was very unusual for her. It is ironic that it is happening now and here in this strange place.

Suddenly she caught another glimpse of movement to her right. She quickly looked in that direction and saw one of the distortions remarkably close to her, 10 or 15 feet away. It was hard to tell since it looked like some sort of energy and was perfectly clear, although this one did appear to have a sort of form to it.

Jessie looked down at her own body again. She still could not quite see it either, but almost. Unlike the other distortions all around her, her own body looked more like clear water or a jelled energy of one sort or another. However, she still felt very solid. "So, why can I see my own body, or at least a more defined form of it, but not whoever belongs to those voices?" she whispered half to herself and the other half to whoever was behind those voices.

She lifted her right arm and tried to look more closely at her hand. The harder she looked at it, the more she could see it solidly formed, yet with the next exhalation of breath, it disappeared completely. She continued to stare at her own hand for what felt like a couple of minutes, trying to bring it into view again, but only barely managing to do so, before losing sight of it again.

Throughout this entire process, she continued to hear birds singing all around her, and the breeze blowing through the leaves in the nearby trees. She could also still hear the laughter of children in the distance. She began to purposefully try to listen to all those sounds while staring at her own hand and just be present. With each passing second her hand seemed to take a more solid form.

She continued to watch this incredible metamorphosis happen right before her eyes. Her hand, nor the rest of her body for that matter, did not feel any different, but it was as though her mind or vision itself was changing to accommodate this new visual reality. She lifted her other hand and looked at it. It was the same as her right one. Both of her hands were quite solid yet perfectly clear. She could clearly see them both and yet see straight through them.

She decided to try touching her hand to her face and see what that felt like. Oddly enough it felt just like it always had. Both her hand and face felt perfectly solid, just how she expected them to feel. However, visually, she was now an entirely clear being.

"Have you ever seen anything so beautiful?" said the voice off to her right again.

Jessie looked in the direction of the voice and to her surprise, she suddenly saw a perfectly formed being standing there, perfectly solid, and yet perfectly clear just like she was.

"Who are you? What is happening here? What is happening to me?"

"I am a Caprician. My name is Allion. Nothing bad is happening to you. You are just taking on our form while you are here in Caprice. It is all very normal, and you are perfectly safe. You can also go back to your world at any time."

"What do you mean 'Go back to my World'? What is this place? I am really confused and a little bit nervous here."

"It's okay, you will understand it all soon enough."

Jessie looked back down at her own body and then back at Allion. She suddenly realized that Allion was not just clear but also seemed to radiate a full spectrum of assorted colors from within, all colors completely independent and yet simultaneously shining, merging to form a very faint but beautiful rainbow and yet still completely clear. She had never seen or even imagined anything like it.

As she stood there trying to calm herself, she realized she could still hear laughter coming from down toward the other end of the lake. "So, there are more of you here?" She said, looking in the direction of the lake.

"Oh yes, there are many of us here and we are all very excited you decided to come join us."

"I am not sure that I 'decided' to come join you. I was at my family reunion looking at a picture and suddenly things started to go a little crazy. The next thing I knew I was here."

"Intentionally or not, you were apparently searching for something, or you would not have found your way here."

"I am not sure what I could have been searching for. Honestly, I was just wasting time looking at some images on the wall. I was not even thinking about anything important when everything started to go crazy."

"What were you thinking about?"

"Honestly?"

"Yes, I always want you to be honest with me. You can tell me anything, absolutely anything. But it will only help you if you are completely honest with me and yourself of course."

"Wait, what do you mean help me?"

"That will come later. So, tell me what you were thinking when the door to Caprice began to open for you?"

Unsure what was happening, she decided to just go with it for now "I was just thinking about how messed up my world is." Jessie said as she shook her head in a sort of self-dismissal.

"In what ways, Jessie?"

"Pretty much every way.

"At that moment, I was thinking how everyone in my family is perfect. They all have nice cars, nice houses, nice jobs, nice everything, except me, and it is not just my family, it is everyone I know. It seems that everyone has their life together except me."

"Why do you feel like that, Jessie? What makes you different from all the people you know? Maybe if we can figure that out, we can figure out what landed you here in Caprice today."

"I Just do not fit in with most people. I do not have any of those things that matter to so many other people in today's world nor do I even have any interest in them. I mean I have a car and an apartment that I like, but they are nothing fancy. I have a job. I make decent money. I like to think I do good things with my work, but just not all that I would like to be able to do. It just seems like everyone else is moving forward in life but with different priorities than I have. Our world is changing dramatically but no one else seems to notice. Sometimes I wonder if it is just me that sees it. But I can see it so clearly, I just cannot understand why other people do not seem to be seeing it."

"What kind of changes are you talking about? What are these things you are seeing?"

"The entire world feels like it is about ready to come apart at the seams. But everyone just seems oblivious to it. The more I am around people, the clearer that becomes. I really hated having to be at that party today with my family."

"I get the feeling you do not like to spend time with your family. Is that true? And if so, why did you have to be around them today?"

"I struggle being around anyone right now. It is not just my family, although sometimes I am afraid they might take it that way. It is people in general that I struggle being around most of the time. But I had to go be around them today because it is the annual family reunion, but we had not had one in a while because of a pandemic that hit our world. If I did not show up, it would have turned into a whole big drama thing, at least with my cousin, so it was easier to just go."

"Why would it have turned into a drama thing?" Allion asked in a very comforting tone of voice.

"I love my cousin. I really do. But we just do not agree on a lot of big issues taking place in the world right now. I am not sure I agree with any people right now, family or otherwise."

Jessie let out a heavy sigh and continued, "However, since she is one of my closest friends and these reunions are especially important to her, she would have been hurt and upset if I did not go. So I went, even though I did not really want to go or even feel truly comfortable in doing so."

Jessie stopped for a moment looking out over the lake and let out another heavy sigh. "It is easier to just show up at some things in today's world and take your chances, than to deal with the hassle of not being there." she continued thoughtfully.

"Why is it 'taking your chances' to go to places in your world?"

"It is risky because the world I come from is overrun with illnesses and disease. We just had a major pandemic that ended up wiping out a huge chunk of our population. The entire world shut down for weeks on end, at various times in different locations, over the last five or six years. Different areas have been reopening and then shutting down again as needed when the virus or other disease becomes too prominent in that area. Even though people do not really talk about it as much as they did, we still have not eradicated it from our world and probably never will. So, everywhere we go, it is a risk we take, especially for people that have any medical issues like compromised immune systems and such. But at the same time, we cannot just sit at home forever. There are safety protocols we can use, but most people do not use them anymore. I try to, but it is so hard in a world where those people who are still trying to survive are the ones that most people look down upon. And that is only the beginning of what is going on in our world."

"What are some of the other things going on in your world?"

Jessie stopped for a minute and a shutter went through her entire being as she thought about all the people that she had lost over the last few years, to the virus, to other diseases and in mass shootings, especially the one at the under privileged school where she works. She shook her head to clear her mind a bit before going on with her story.

"You can talk to me Jessie. You are safe here. We are all so extremely glad you decided to come for a visit and want to learn all about you and your world."

"Who are you again and why are you so interested in my life and where I am from? What am I doing here?" She looked around again and realized that everything seemed to be even more solid than it was just a few minutes ago.

"Well, Jessie, I am the leader here in Caprice. We have a wonderful place here and I am incredibly happy to share it with you. You are here now because you chose to take this path. We felt your pain and knew you were crying out for help in your own way. So, we opened the door for you and you, although hesitantly, walked through it.

No one is ever forced to come here, and no one can even make it through the portal if they are not ready, willing, and able to do so. You can also return to your world at any time you want."

"Wait a minute. How was I crying out for help? I just wanted to get through the family reunion and head back home as soon as possible. Then I wound up here. I do not even know where here is. Am I hallucinating? Did I die or pass out, hit my head, and go into a coma or something? I do not understand how I got here, and I sure do not understand how I can go back home whenever I want."

"It might be hard to understand right now, but as I said before, you can truly leave anytime you wish. Please know that you are not trapped here by any means. We really do hope you will stay for a bit though. Everyone here would really like to spend time with you and get to know you better."

"Who is everyone?" Jessie looked around but still did not see anyone else. "I do not see anyone, but you and I use the term 'see" in a very liberal sense here." Jessie said with a quick glance back at Allion hoping to at least see Him a bit more clearly.

"Just relax, take a deep breath, and look around again. There are other people here that love and care about you as well. Listen. Love is all around you."

Jessie suddenly became aware of the sounds she had heard before of laughter and people talking. She tried to look around again and back toward the lake but still did not see anyone. The sounds were getting a little louder with each passing moment.

She thought to herself that maybe they were all farther around the lake, even though she could see clearly all the way around it and could not see anyone else anywhere in sight. Maybe if she walked a little closer to the sounds, she would be able to see more of these clear beings like Allion.

About the same time that her thoughts formed in her head, she realized that she was no longer sitting on the rock but rather moving to her left around the lake with no effort on her part whatsoever. She seemed to be slowly floating, although she could still feel her feet planted firmly but lightly on the ground.

She looked to her right and sure enough this Allion being was floating right next to her. Jessie felt a little twinge of dizziness and even a little nausea. She closed her eyes for a moment and opened them again. At least the feeling of nausea then completely disappeared. She looked over toward the lake and felt a sense of peace rush over her again.

The water was so perfectly clear she could see every stone and every fish swimming about in it all the way out to the point where the reflections of the beautiful clouds above covered what was underneath the surface.

Allion sighed and said, "Ah, isn't it just so beautiful?"

"Yes, it really is."

Then she heard one of those voices right next to her on her left side. She turned to see who was talking to her and there was no one there.

"Oh, this again?" she said shaking her head.

"What?"

"Why are you guys so hard to see?"

"Simply because we do not have a physical form like you are used to seeing. So, it takes a little getting used to and a little practice to be able to see us clearly. For example, Sarah is just to your left. Jessie, I would like you to meet Sarah. She is one of the Capricians that calls this place home."

Jessie looked to her left but of course did not see anything.

A very cheerful voice practically sang out next to her. "Hi, Jessie. I am so glad to meet you and even happier you came to visit us. I know it takes a bit of getting used to, but it sure is beautiful, isn't it? Just wait until you see the sun setting behind the lake and then watch thousands of stars slowly come out of hiding in the sky overhead. There is nothing like it!"

"I am glad to meet you too." Jessie said hesitantly not wanting to look in the direction of the voice. "Forgive me for being a little freaked out here."

Jessie glanced out over the lake and then cut her eyes back in the direction of the voice. This time she thought she could almost make out another form. Where the first one, Allion, looked more like pure energy, this one appeared more like truly clear water, much like the lake. She tried to wrap her mind around this somehow. She tried to compare it to the lake. She knew the water was there and yet she could see straight through it. Maybe it is all some sort of illusion. Jessie kept trying to see her better but felt quite awkward looking at her. She could not tell if this Sarah person was looking back at her or not. Jessie found herself looking her up and down trying to see something solid. However, that felt very awkward and rude, so she decided to look back out over the lake.

"So how many of you are there here?"

Sarah answered, "I have lost count, and it is always changing, but today, you are the most important person here."

Jessie looked back toward Sarah and could suddenly see her well enough to know she was looking at her and smiling.

"I think you all might have gotten me mixed up with someone else. I really did not plan to visit. Like I said, it just sort of happened and trust me, I am no one special."

"You are incredibly special to us Jessie McCallin. Why do you feel like you are not?"

"Oh my gosh, where should I start? My life is a mess. The world I live in is a mess. Everything seems completely out of control, especially my own life. It is overwhelming to even think about it. Nothing at all like this place here seems to be. This is amazing. If there is a place like this in my world, I want to find it."

"Maybe we can help you with some of that here."

"How can you do that?"

"Well, that is what we sort of specialize in here." Allion said as he winked at Sarah.

She smiled back and then said to Jessie, "Come go for a walk with us."

Suddenly, the three of them began moving together around the lake without any effort at all on Jessie's part. This was such a weird sensation, but she was starting to get the hang of it. She sure liked feeling lighter on her feet. She also suddenly realized that her sprained foot she got playing with her neighbor's dog last week, was not hurting at all anymore either. In fact, nothing on her entire body was hurting at all. She just enjoyed that feeling for what seemed like several minutes, but it was apparently only a minute or two since they had not progressed far at all around the lake during that time. Even as disconcerting as it was, she thought to herself, "Maybe this is heaven." She allowed her mind to wander deeper into this world, almost forgetting about the other beings until one of them spoke to her again.

"Tell me more about your world Jessie." Allion's voice startled her and brought her back to the moment at hand. He had such a gentle, soft voice, it put Jessie at ease, which was a little weird for her, as usually no one's voice ever put her at ease these days. Something was vastly different here. These people were different. She was different just being here.

## MAKING A DECISION

Jessie thought to herself for a moment. "Maybe I am having this experience to work through part of the stuff going on with me. It is very unlikely that any of this is real anyway, so I might as well just go through the process and get it all out there. Maybe a resolution of some sort here will resolve this whole situation back in the real world too."

Jessie began the process. "It is nothing like this place appears to be, I can tell you that. It used to feel far more peaceful than it is now. In my world today there is nothing but absolute chaos.

Our world is plagued with so many diseases and illnesses that it is not even safe to leave the house anymore. There is civil unrest and chaos everywhere from big cities to small rural towns like where I live and everywhere in between. I used to love what a diverse nation I lived in, but it has started to rip apart at the seams. The entire world has, not just my area, but around the entire globe. The environment is getting worse by the day with no end or solution in sight. Every year the heat waves are becoming more unbearable. We have an ever-growing number of places on earth that are just no longer compatible with human life. We have immense wildfires that are often just left to burn out of control. Everywhere you look there are floods, mudslides, earthquakes, tsunamis, droughts, and such. It just never ends. Food shortages are worse than they have ever been before. Crime rates are through the roof. Mass shootings are a daily occurrence somewhere in my world. It is not even safe to go to the grocery store and often not worth the risk to go. It is harder and harder to find all the items you need when you do go and if they are available, they are harder to afford. Then assuming you can afford them, they are less and less safe to even eat when you get it all home. Every time you turn on the news, there is a new war or conflict somewhere or a new disease or an old one making a historic comeback. War just continues to spread even more rapidly than diseases. There are more people hungry than not. My world is just absolutely falling apart."

"All of that sounds incredibly stressful. I hate that your planet is like that. What about your own personal world Jessie?"

"It is a mess too. How could it not be with the rest of the world falling apart."

"What specifically brought you here today?"

"I have no idea how I even got here, so not sure how to answer that."

"Where are you personally in this whole scheme of things in your world?"

"I personally struggle with wondering how the world got into this mess. I feel like this is not how it was supposed to be and yet it just keeps getting worse and I do not understand it."

"How do you think it was supposed to be?"

"The creator in our world started it out as a sort of paradise where we were all supposed to live happily ever after, but that very quickly went wrong. The first of my kind succumbed to temptation and very quickly turned the whole thing into a mess."

"Do you think it could ever be resolved and turned back into its initial purpose?"

"Probably not. It feels like it has gone too far downhill to ever go back to how it was supposed to be. We have literally destroyed so much of the earth itself that a lot of our scientists are saying we are already past the point of no return."

"That is a shame. I hate to hear that. Do you like what you see so far here in Caprice?"

"Of course, I love it. I have never seen any place as beautiful. The sky, the water, the very air that we are breathing, feels so fresh and clean. It is odd because I feel so very alive and healthy here, but I am not sure that I am not actually dead or in a coma in my own world."

"You are definitely not dead or even in a coma."

"Then what is this place and how did I get here?"

"This is Caprice. Our home. A world that we chose to make what it is today. Many years ago, our world was in just as bad a situation as yours is today. We made decisions that turned it all around and now it is the beautiful paradise that you see, feel, hear, and smell."

"Whatever decisions you made certainly seems to have worked then." Jessie looked around again and smiled.

She then looked down at the ground and her smile faded.

'What is the matter, Jessie?" Allion asked with such a loving and genuine sounding voice, Jessie felt at complete ease with him.

"I was just thinking about my world. It would take a lot more than deciding to change, for anything to improve there. Besides, the people in charge there would never make those kinds of decisions even if they were offered to them."

Jessie lost herself for a moment, then continued, "I cannot say much though. I am unable to fix my own life to be more like I want it to be either."

"What is going on in your life that you would like to change, Jessie? Maybe they are all somehow interconnected."

"I don't know about that. I am not actually involved enough in the world around me for decisions I make to have any effect on anyone else around me."

"We are all far more connected than we think we are in most cases." Allion continued "I really would like to hear more about your life as well."

Jessie thought for a moment. She usually did not share much about her own life with anyone. But what could it hurt to share here in this fantasy world that she must have somehow created within her own mind? Maybe it would even help somehow. Her life was quite a mess and if there was a chance to figure any of it out, why not give it a try. She just did not know who these people might be or if she could trust them at all. On the other hand, she did not know if she had any other choice at this point. She might as well go along with it.

## JESSIE'S WORLD

As if sensing her hesitation, Allion gently said, "It's okay, Jessie, to share anything you want here."

"Well, I do feel like my personal life is quite a mess. I hate my job more every day. I used to feel like I made more of a difference in the world, at least in the world of some children, especially when I can place them in new safer homes. However, now there are so many more children than there are homes. Especially with the amount of people that died in the pandemic as well as other diseases that are so rampant everywhere you look, more children are being displaced every day. Homelessness is at an all-time high, especially among children, and I feel helpless to do anything at all about it. I feel like I am constantly stirring the pot with all of it, without ever really accomplishing much of anything."

"I see. I understand how frustrating that would be. Anything else?"

Hesitantly, she continued. "Financially, life is a struggle as well for me. I end up, for the most part, living payday to payday. However, I cannot quit this job cos there is no one to take my place and I cannot leave the few children I can help high and dry. So, it is an ongoing process there too."

Allion spoke softly, "Money can certainly complicate things. People get so caught up in it. We used to have a saying here, "The love of money is the root of all evil."

"We still have that saying in our world and I imagine always will until it all implodes on itself one day."

"You might be surprised at how quickly things can change sometimes. Anything else going on with you personally?"

I also have this auto immune thing going on so that I constantly have pain somewhere in my body that even the doctors cannot figure out a way to get rid of. That is a big one for me. There are other less important things but those are the ones that cause the most chaos in my life and in the world around me."

"So, if you could change one thing about your life, what would it be Jessie?"

Jessie took a moment and thought about it. "More manageability. My life is so out of control and seems completely unmanageable a great deal of the time. Not just my life personally, but the entire world seems unmanageable. So, if I could figure out a way to make things in my life and the world around me a bit more manageable, that would be a miracle for sure. Right now, it is all out of control."

"I can help you with that." Allion smiled at Jessie, and she felt a small sense of peace being around other people for the first time in many years.

Jessie had almost forgotten about Sarah on the other side of her until she spoke. "I would like to help you with that as well Jessie, if you would like me too."

"Absolutely, I will take any help I can get and what do I have to lose at this point."

## TRUE NATURE OF THINGS

"As I said when you first got here. We are so glad you came here. You are exactly where you are supposed to be."

Jessie had no idea how anyone could help her with all her problems and help her figure out how to get her life back in order, especially with the world in the mess it is in, but she was certainly willing to listen to their ideas. After all, what did she have to lose?

Jessie continued talking more in depth about her world as if the contrast was becoming more evident by the moment. "If I lived in a world like this, it would not be hard to be happy. Everything is so beautiful here. You two seem genuinely nice and caring. I can hear others laughing and they seem so happy. The people in my world are so caught up in politics, money and fighting with each other, true happiness is quite elusive. Many of the people are downright mean, evil I would venture to say. Wars and crime are rampant everywhere you look. Terrorism, illness, poverty, civil unrest, disease, suicide, mental illness, corrupt politicians, and I could go on and on about it all. It is a horrible world. Even the good parts of it, like the parks and such are shrinking by the day, and we are, as a species, destroying all the world's resources. Pollution is so overpowering that the earth cannot even sustain itself much longer. I am constantly saying that it feels like our entire world is coming unglued."

"Sounds like your world needs a bit of divine help."

"I personally am not interested in talking about religion. That sparks too much controversy with people where I am from. I think most people in religions, at least the ones you hear about the most, are some of the worst hypocrites out there. I grew up in a church as well as household where I felt like everything I did and every thought I had, even as a small child, was going to send me straight to hell, at least any of those thoughts or actions that contradicted any of the authority figures in my life."

"So, you have never been interested in religion at all? Do you even believe in God?"

"I have always had an interest in both really. I do believe in God and always have but have always struggled with religion. I am not sure I believe in religion as much as I do God. Does it sound weird to believe in God but not religion?" Jessie glanced at both Sarah and Allion and realized they were both smiling back at her. They were both easier to see now than they were just a few minutes ago.

Allion smiled and said, "God and religion are not the same things. We get that all the time. I always like to remind people that God did not create all the different religions, people did. God just created everything else." Sarah and Allion both laughed so genuinely that it made Jessie laugh as well.

Sarah continued to press Jessie a bit about her faith and beliefs. "So, tell us a bit more about your experience with both."

"I have tried many times over the years to find a church that I could join and truly feel a part of, but it just never seems to work out that way. There always seems to be too many people in the church that are far more interested in playing

God themselves rather than helping others to find God's love. Those churches might be out there, but I do not think I have ever found one."

Jessie paused for a moment to gauge the reactions of Allion and Sarah before continuing, "The majority of churches out there seem, in my experience, to be more interested in judging everyone else and thinking they know more than anyone in any other religion other than their own. It just never made sense to me that there would only be one church that had all the answers and yet all the churches out there thought they were that one church. If they truly were THE church, why did God not bless them in some way so they could show the world, they really were THAT church. There are just too many of them claiming to be the only true church. There is no way they could all be right, so are they all wrong? Who knows? I just never felt as though any of them really had what it took to truly be that one true church that they all claimed to be. Luckily for me, it was not really a closeness to the church that I was looking for but rather a closeness to God Himself."

"Where did you most feel that closeness if not in church?"

"The times that I have felt the closest to God was when I was out in nature. I mean I felt a closeness to Him at various times at different churches as well, at least occasionally, but I always feel close to God when I am out in nature. I am sure other people feel that closeness in church a lot more than I did, just for me, it was so much more profound and powerful in nature."

Jessie's thoughts flashed back to a very tense Sunday 35 or so years ago. She was just 8 years old at the time and her own inner voice was just beginning to find its way into the world. It did not go so well that day and that was only the beginning of a lifelong struggle with expressing her inner most thoughts about God, especially in relation to the world around her.

## HOPE

"A penny for your thoughts Jessie." Sarah's words gently brought Jessie back to the here and now.

"I was thinking back to my childhood church and remembering some of the things that happened there."

"Anything you would care to share?'

Jessie thought for a moment and decided to share one quick story. "Maybe this will give you all some insight into how it all started for me as far as my conflict about religion."

Allion and Sarah glanced at each other, smiled, and looked at Jessie again, then Sarah said, "Yes, do tell."

"The time I was just thinking about was when I was about 8 years old. My parents and I were at our family church. It just so happened that day we had a guest minister visit from a neighboring town. He was an extremely well-liked youth pastor and the leader of a popular contemporary Christian band. I knew who he was but had never met him personally before. Anyway, he led our

Sunday School class that morning and of all things, the topic he chose was hell. Yes, hell fire and brimstone with a bunch of second graders. Well, after Sunday School was over, we all went back out to adult church together. As he was getting ready to give his main sermon, he started by calling each of the kids from our earlier class up to the front of the church. He asked each one of us a question. Each time it was a different question to which all the other kids gave a quick short reply and then seemed proud to receive his praise for repeating what he had said in class. When he called me up, things took a turn for the worse, at least for him, and very shortly afterwards, the entire church. When he began his question to me, he meant to ask me what he had taught us that morning in class about hell itself, but instead he asked what I personally believed about hell. My answer was not what anyone expected, nor was it an answer that would soon be forgotten by anyone in attendance."

Jessie hesitated because she never really knew how anyone would take this story, so she rarely shared it.

Sarah encouraged Jessie to continue, "I bet this is going to be good." Sarah laughed, leaned a bit toward Jessie and said, "What did you say?"

"I took the microphone, stepped away from him, looked at the crowd, and began a monologue as quickly as I could because I knew they were going to take the microphone away from me as soon as they realized what I was about to say. In my most authoritative 8-year-old voice, I said, "I am glad someone finally asked me that question. I have to say, I am not sure why a God that is supposed to be so loving, kind and creative, one so wise as to create the entire earth and all of the animals and people on it, all of which He then calls His children, would then choose to send some of them, most of them it seems, to such a burning hell as we talked about this morning and all because they did even the smallest things wrong."

Jessie looked over at Allion to see if she could read his semi-visible expressions to gauge whether to finish the story. He was smiling at her from ear to ear, as if almost ready to laugh out loud at this scenario she was laying out before them. With a new excitement in her voice, she continued. "Of course, by the time I finished that sentence, the minister had decided to take away the mic, so I began to run toward the podium as I continued. 'I am just an 8-year-old little kid, but I have an aquarium at home with all kinds of little animals in it. If I can catch them, they go in it. Sometimes, they do not all get along. If one of the animals starts hurting, killing, or even eating the other animals, I immediately take them out of the tank and do not allow them back in it. I do not, however, take them in the house and put them in the fireplace and slowly burn them forever. I simply remove them from the little world I have created in my space in my dad's shop and do not allow them back in it. I believe that is what God does when we do not follow Him or His Son. He removes us from his Kingdom. I cannot believe that such a loving God would burn his own creations forever, just because they messed up for a little while here on earth. An eternity in burning hell, for one or two small mistakes here in this temporary life. I just do not get it. Maybe that could be the case for something big, but not for every little thing that we do that someone else in church might think is wrong.'

By that time, the minister was chasing me around the podium as the wire got wrapped around it more and more. I continued as fast as I could. 'I think God is far more loving, forgiving and kind than that, so I really don't think most of you actually know God, at least not the same one I do, or you would talk about Him more and less about hell.' About that time, the minister was able to pull the wire on the microphone and take it away from me. So, I screamed out. 'I promise you all this, I will go and find out who God really is and come back and let you all know one day.'

By that point, my parents had both gotten up and headed down the side isle toward the front of the church, so I ran down the center isle and out the back door. I knew I was in the most trouble I had ever been in before in my life. I also knew I had just spoken my most deep-felt truth and I that meant every word of it."

"What happened after that?" Sarah asked, seeming genuinely curious.

"Let's just say, nothing was ever quite the same afterwards. That church we went to ended up splitting up because half of the parishioners wanted to head in the direction of talking more about the love of God and all that He gives and offers us daily, about His forgiveness and all that He wants for us and to do so in a more positive atmosphere, while the other half felt it was more important to tell people what would happen to them if they didn't follow the rules. My immediate family never actually went back to either of those two churches afterwards. So, I guess you can say that any chance I had of being any sort of spiritual leader of any kind went out the door the same day I proclaimed I would do it."

Allion and Sarah again smiled at each other and then at Jessie. She suddenly realized she had been holding her breath since she finished that last sentence. She slowly let it out but did not say another word.

## BACK TO BASICS

Sarah gently encouraged her to continue, "It sounds like you have always had a close relationship with God even if not with religion."

"I am not sure that I would describe it as a close relationship. Most of my life, I have felt as though I was far more interested in being closer to God than He was to me."

"Why do you feel that way Jessie?" Allion asked.

"It just feels like I have spent a good deal of time trying to learn about God and He seems to have spent little time trying to get close to me. I totally get that about religion and God not being the same thing. But if God is not in religion, then how are most people supposed to find out about him, her, whatever?"

"That is a good question, Jessie. Different people are able to learn about God in different ways." Sarah said.

They both looked at Allion, He nodded as if acknowledging her question but without answering or replying at all.

The three of them stood there for what felt like two or three minutes looking out over the lake. Jessie closed her eyes and concentrated on the sounds of children laughing. She opened her eyes again and looked down at the water's edge. Suddenly, there they were, children of all different ages running around, playing, laughing, chasing each other, and having a wonderful time. Jessie smiled and looked at Sarah and then Allion. They both realized she had finally seen the children.

After what seemed like 5 more minutes or so, but was probably much less, Allion spoke to Jessie again.

"So, Jessie, I would love to hear in your own words what you personally believe about God now that you are older. It sounds like you have always had strong feelings about the things you do believe. Would you care to share anymore?"

"I am not sure. I want to believe in God, but I want to believe in a loving, kind, generous, caring God, not just the vindictive, wrathful, angry God that causes so much pain and suffering in the world."

"Have you ever personally had any of those experiences with God yourself?"

"I am not sure. Of course, as a kid I grew up in church, as I said, and wanted to please God. However, I was always taught that there were so many rules and obligations I just never thought I would be able to live up to any of them. I look around and see all the beautiful creations and think God must lean more toward the caring side, but there is just so much wrong in the world too. It is so confusing and quite honestly, most often, terrifying to think about, especially combined with what most of the people I know seem to think. Then I add all of that to the times that we are living through right now. It is all just very scary and at times I am just not sure what to believe about God or any of it."

Allion continued, "Let us start there. What is it that you are most afraid that God is?"

"I am most afraid that He is just a wrathful, mean, vindictive God that is out to get humankind and that just wants to make everyone pay for their sins and end up dying and going to hell. I believe He is Himself very righteous and if He demands the same of his followers, there is no one else in existence, on earth at least, that can really live up to His expectations. My biggest fear is that all those people from my childhood were right, and we are all going straight to hell."

"Okay, Fair enough. Next question. What do you most hope God is?"

"Well, I hope that He is a far more loving God than that. I hope that once Jesus came and died for our sins, that it opened a door for us to be forgiven of our sins, if we ask and then follow Him. I hope that we now have a way to have eternal life and not be condemned to eternal hell, if we choose a good and righteous path."

"What would that look like to you personally? How would it affect your life if you found out that God was indeed that loving, kind, forgiving God that you hope He is? How would it change your personal relationship to Him?"

"Well, I would probably spend more time in church, or at least in prayer for sure." Jessie said with a small chuckle, then continued thoughtfully. "I would definitely be more interested in pursuing a closer relationship with Him and giving it a harder try to live up to His standards if I felt like I had a better chance of being part of His kingdom and knew that He was in fact a more loving and kinder God."

"I see."

No one said anything else for a while and gave Jessie time to complete her thoughts.

A short while later Allion continued, "So, we know what you fear God is and we know what you hope God is, what do you truly believe in your heart that He is?"

After she paused for a couple more moments, she then added, "I suppose somewhere in between. I think God does need to be just and fair having rules and organization to prevent the mass chaos like I see in my world, but at the same time, offer us a way to have all the wonderful blessings that He has offered us from day one."

"I am not sure I could have said that better myself." Allion chuckled and looked at Sarah then back at Jessie.

"It is just so hard to see beyond all the hypocrisy in so many of the churches and religions out there. I know there are a lot of people in each of them that are sincere and are genuinely interested in doing God's will and sharing His love. I feel quite sure there are some great churches out there. However, those kinds of places are not the ones that are most often in the public eye. That kind of love and commitment to God is not what most people see in them unfortunately. Many people also equate the most prominent people they see in religion to God Himself. I just wish there were a better way to distinguish the two. Being a true believer in God's greatness and the possibilities that He offers must go a lot deeper than a few hours in church each week and trying not to curse publicly or get caught doing something much worse."

'I can promise you it is a lot deeper than that."

'How do you know for sure?" Jessie asked genuinely interested once again in who these beings were before her.

"Let's just say I know a thing or two about the God here in Caprice and how that relates to the God in your world as well." Sarah gave Jessie such a sweet smile that it instantly put her at total ease.

At that precise moment, Jessie realized she could see her very clearly now and how beautiful she was. It was as if she could see her very essence, more than any sort of physical appearance. Jessie felt herself smiling back at her.

"So, what is the God like here in Caprice?"

Sarah looked over at Allion and back at Jessie and said, "Let me take a stab at this one. Our God here is all those things you hoped for in God and more. He is patient, kind, wise, has a genuine sense of humor and loves all His children, no matter how old or young they are. He is a great friend and someone that any of us here can talk to about anything. When we pray to

Him, He listens carefully, whether there is just one of us praying to him or a whole bunch of us at once. It feels as though everything in the universe stops for that moment and He gives us his full attention."

Sarah paused for a moment then stretched out her arms and said, "Look at all of this." She motioned all around them, then up to the sky, down toward the grass, out across the lake and then back to Jessie. "He made all these wonderful things for us to enjoy. The trees, animals, sky, water, all the people, all the food, the warmth of the sun, everything that you can see, hear, or feel here, He made, and He made it all because of His love for us."

"This is a beautiful place for sure. But what about the rules? What happens if you break the rules? Are you kicked out of here or what happens?"

"The rules here are amazingly simple. We must be honest and open. We must love our neighbors and always choose kindness over anger, selfishness, pride, or resentment. We try to be happy with our life as well as be genuinely happy for our neighbors or friends when they have successes in their life. We are never envious or spiteful toward others. When we have a goal, we strive for it and ask for help when we need it but are willing to do most of the work ourselves to reach it."

"Sounds wonderful, but what about when you have a disagreement? What about wars or crime here?"

"We really do not have any war or crime here. There is enough of everything we need to go around. No one has an excess amount of anything, but we all have everything that we need or want. We do not have a currency system here either. There is no need for it. If we have a need or even a want, we just put it out there, ask God for it, let our neighbors know about it, work for it and somehow it always seems to come to us. If our desire is of a pure spirit and we want it out of sincerity because we would enjoy it and it would bring happiness to ourselves, our family, or our friends. We never try to outdo others or have more than another just for the sake of being better than them. If we have extra of something that someone else wants or needs, we share it with them, knowing that there will always be enough to go around. Disagreeing about something is not wrong, if we take it as such, respect each other and move on with our life without getting angry or trying to force the other people to believe the same way we do."

Jessie listened to those words and thought again for a moment that all of this had to be a dream, but it felt so real. She closed her eyes and could hear the children's laughter off in the distance and back toward the meadow. She subconsciously turned to look toward them again and there they were, even more than before, at least a dozen more small children running and playing and chasing each other around the field, having even more fun than before. A couple of older looking children were swinging one of the younger ones back and forth between their arms and the laughter of that child was beyond contagious. Just hearing those giggles made Jessie want to laugh aloud as well. She felt so at ease, unlike with the children back at the family reunion, where she felt so self-conscious about being around them. Here it was just pure joy with no fear or discomfort of any kind.

Sarah continued as if she knew what Jessie was thinking. "It really is quite amazing to see the children here. They grow up so happy and content. They never have to deal with sickness, poverty, war, or any of the things that the children in your world must deal with."

Jessie tried to imagine a world like that, then compared that to her world. "That is incredible. There are more children hungry and in poor health in my world than there are otherwise. It is heartbreaking really."

Sarah tried to comfort her. "It does not have to be that way. There is none of that here. No one ever goes hungry, and the taste of the food is amazing. It is also grown right here in our little area of Caprice and in abundance. We have food year-round growing in our gardens and anyone who wants anything to eat can just go and harvest what they want at any time. So, it is always fresh as well. We do not use any fertilizers, pesticides, insecticides, or anything of that sort, so everything is healthy for us and for all the animals that also feed off the vegetables and other plants here."

Jessie thought about that for a moment and shook her head.

"What is it, Jessie?"

"Back in my world, even the food that we do have is not healthy to eat anymore. It is full of all kinds of chemicals, or one thing or another. There are constant food recalls. I just do not even feel safe most of the time going to the store to buy food. We must eat to live, but most of the food that we eat is also what is killing us. Our health care facilities and hospitals are at capacity most of the time. We have so many people sick with heart disease, diabetes, obesity, cancer, debilitating arthritis, arterial diseases, Alzheimer's. I could go on about it all day and not cover it all. It is just unreal and completely out of control."

Allion agreed with Sarah and tried to comfort Jessie. "I am sorry that your world is impacted in that way. That is not how people are supposed to live. This world is set up with the perfect number of pollinators of all kinds, birds, bats, bees, other insects and even the wind itself. We have different climates and weather patterns here that also allow for different food items to grow in different areas. Each location is set up with supporting non-edible plants that help enrich the environment and wildlife, so that it is all in perfect harmony. We are careful not to introduce plants in one area that will mess up the ecological or environmental stability of that area. We do not have any of those diseases that you mentioned here. Our people are made healthier by the foods they eat, the air they breathe and the water they drink. I cannot wait to show you our world here and how it works."

Jessie smiled and said, "I cannot wait to see it."

"Speaking of food," Allion added, "It is about time for dinner I believe. You must be hungry. Would you like to join us for an amazing meal that I am sure you will enjoy? We would certainly love your company."

"I would love to. I do have a couple of food allergies and issues that I must be careful of though. I am also trying to be vegetarian but still struggling with that somewhat. I hope none of those are an issue."

"No worries, you will fit in perfectly fine here." Sarah smiled and took Jessie by the hand and started to lead her toward the edge of the woods. Suddenly, they were on a path that circled around behind the woods and led to a beautiful little cottage with a gorgeous front lawn. A dozen or so of these Caprician beings were already there setting up an array of food on a couple of picnic tables on the front lawn. Before Jessie could even take it all in, they were there in the middle of it all.

"Grab a plate and dig in. Don't be shy, take all you want to eat. It is all perfectly healthy, organic, and even vegan." She handed Jessie a plate and took one for herself as she led the way around the table. "Oh, and don't worry too much about your food allergies. I think you will find that they will not be a problem here."

Jessie could not help but smile at all that food. She did feel a bit hungry. The more she looked at and smelled all that food, the hungrier she felt. It all looked so bright and colorful, she could not help but want a bite or two of everything.

She filled her plate up to the point that she was almost embarrassed. She looked around to see if anyone noticed how full she had filled her plate. No one was watching or paying any attention to her at all as they were all just as anxiously digging into all the dishes themselves and her plate looked a little bare compared to many of theirs. That made Jessie smile on the inside as well as the outside.

Just as she started to look around to see where she wanted to sit, a young girl that looked about 9 years old walked up to her and said, "Excuse me Ma'am, would you like to come sit with me?"

Jessie felt a bit anxious but also relieved. She hated being in situations where she had to choose for herself where to sit in public places like this. At least this young girl seemed polite and interested in spending time with her so she would go with it for now. She started to follow the girl toward her chosen table when the little girl said, "don't forget your drink." Jessie picked up a glass of what she believed to be lemonade from the nearest table and followed the little girl to a beautiful picnic table overlooking the valley below.

"My name is Gracie. You were talking to my mom earlier. Isn't she the best?"

"Hi Gracie. My name is Jessie and yes, your mom seems like an impressive lady."

Gracie smiled up at her and said, "So, what is your favorite thing about Caprice so far? The little girl asked this with what seemed to be very genuine curiosity.

Jessie was caught off guard a bit by this question and before she could answer, everyone sitting around all the tables suddenly shouted out together. "Thank you, God, for this amazing food. Here, Here."

Little Gracie followed it up with her own "Amen." And then looked back at Jessie. "Sorry about the interruption. Just gotta give credit where credit is due, eh? So, what is your favorite thing so far?"

Even though she was still caught off guard a little, she was happy to realize there were a lot of things she really liked about this place, even the people. However, to think of just one thing so far would be hard.

"That is a good question. I might have to think about that for a little bit. What about you? What is your favorite thing?"

Without any hesitation, Gracie started talking quite fast and Jessie could tell she was so happy about sharing this with her. "I love the birds best, I think. They are so awesome. Did you know there is a heron down by the lake that lets me feed him grapes from my hand? I just love him so much and he loves me too and of course he loves grapes too." She said this with excitement that only a young child could have about something like that. Although thinking about it a moment longer, Jessie had to admit that she would be quite excited as well to hand feed a heron.

"That must be cool. I think I would love to do that as well."

"You can, any time. He is almost always down there. We just call him Henry, but I am sure he will come by any name you would like to call him.

If you have grapes, he doesn't care. There are also a lot of ducks, geese, and deer that hang out down by the lake as well. There are bears that come by each evening and clean off the dishes that everyone leaves out for them after dinner. They are so fun to watch too. They especially love pumpkin pie!"

"Wait a minute, you feed the bears here?" Jessie asked with a bit of a scare.

"Oh yes of course, We all love doing it. There is plenty for them to eat in the fields too but just between you and I, they really love my mom's cooking as much as I do!"

"That doesn't cause them to get too close to people or cause any problems?"

"Oh no, not at all. Why would it?" Gracie asked with total innocence. "Sometimes the deer come over and nudge them out of the way if there is pie. They all love pumpkin pie! But there is always enough for everyone. We all have animals we feed each evening and sometimes at other times during the day. Pretty much anytime we make a big meal, we put out all the leftovers for the animals. It is just what we do." She said with a smile, shrugged her shoulders and then trailed off into another conversation about her favorite kind of butterflies and how there is a tree out back where all the monarchs hang out.

Jessie was still a bit anxious about the whole bear story but directed her attention back to Gracie. "If you walk under the tree, they will all flutter about and fly up into the air. But then they settle back down and if you lay still in the grass, they will land all over you. It kind of tickles but is so much fun. Maybe you could do that with me tomorrow or sometime."

"I would love to. Its sounds amazing."

"Excellent. I will come find you and we will go do it."

Jessie heard a familiar voice behind her. "So, you have met my daughter?"

"Oh, she is such a delight."

"Yes, she is, even if I do say so myself." Sarah smiled and looked down at her daughter.

"What do you think of the food? Did you get enough to eat?"

"Oh, my goodness, you should have seen how full my plate was to start with. I think that was the best meal I have ever had! If I ate that much in my world, I would be feeling a bit rough by now and would have probably already gained about 10lbs." They both laughed.

"Well, you do not have to worry about either of those things here. "

"I am not sure I can finish it all though. My eyes were bigger than my stomach."

"No worries. Nothing goes to waste here. See those dishes over there?" she pointed over by the edge of the yard and there were all these beautiful platters sitting lined up along the edge of a little stream that Jessie had not noticed before. "We just put all our scrapes over there and the animals come and eat it all up by the evening usually. I am sure Gracie mentioned something about that." She smiled and winked at her daughter.

"Yes, she did." Jessie said and smiled at her as well.

"Whenever you are sure you have finished your meal and shared your leftovers, you can just put your plate on the picnic table there next to the creek. Then I would love it if you would meet me down by the gazebo." She pointed to the other side of the yard, back the way they had come. "There is something I want to show you."

Jessie nodded and said, "I will see you there momentarily." Sarah smiled and hurried off down toward the gazebo.

Jessie finished the last few bites that she could fit in, took the scrapes over and felt a little guilty but excited at the same time to be purposefully feeding wildlife. That practice was highly frowned upon in most cases back in her world.

She took her plate over to the table and asked a woman standing there, if she could help do the dishes. Smiling, the woman said, "You are a guest and you have just got to go see what Sarah wants to show you." She used both arms to shoo Jessie off in that direction. Jessie was not sure how this woman knew about that but hurried off just the same.

As Jessie walked over toward the Gazebo, she suddenly realized that her anxiety level was the lowest it had been in years. Normally if she would have to do something in front of other people, even walking across this field, her anxiety level would have been through the roof. Maybe it was because she was not totally sure she was even here. Maybe it was just a dream or hallucination after all or at least she still had that in the back of her mind.

She continued to walk toward the gazebo and decided to just be in the present and enjoy this state of being for the moment, before she woke up or whatever might happen that would end this trip to paradise, even if only in her own mind.

As she neared the gazebo, she noticed more people lined up all around the field and down by the lake. This really caught Jessie's attention. She wondered what they all were waiting to see.

She heard Sarah call out to her, "Jessie, over here." As she drew closer Sarah said, "I am sure you have seen some amazing sunsets in your world, but this one, promises to be one of the most spectacular you, or maybe any of us, have ever seen." She said looking down toward the lake. Jessie followed her gaze and the lake still looked perfectly blue with big white fluffy clouds reflecting in it and the sun was still a short distance from the horizon. In Jessie's world, they would still have another half hour or so at least before the sun would tip down behind the mountains. She wondered if it happened quicker here.

Jessie looked at Sarah and smiled as Sarah started sharing her excitement of the sunset with her. "Part of the enjoyment I get from this is watching all the people make their way to their favorite spot to watch it. Pretty much everyone here stops whatever they are doing and walks down to the meadow or the lake or up on a mountain or wherever they feel inspired that day to watch the sunset. Once they settle down, they all share a bit with those around them about their day. They usually turn to their neighbor and tell them what their favorite thing about their day was and then they ask their neighbor their favorite in turn. I just love watching all the people gather seeing they are so happy, and it brings such joy to know that all those people are at one time engaged in gratitude and ending their day with such deliberate happiness and kindness. I just love Caprice. Don't you?"

Jessie nodded and turned her attention back to the crowd gathering below. She could hear the chatter floating slowly up the hill to where they stood. How impressive to know every utterance was that of happiness. Then someone exclaimed loudly, "Here she goes!" and there was a collective sigh that rang out across the valley.

Suddenly the sky looked as though it were about to catch on fire. Color exploded across the sky in such brilliance that it seemed just as otherworldly as the Capricians themselves did to Jessie.

The colors reflected so dramatically in the lake below that it seriously looked like the lake had turned into a beautiful, living, breathing, incredible art display. Jessie heard herself gasp. She truly had never seen a sunset so incredible in her life. And by the sound of the people around her, neither had they.

As the sun slowly faded behind the mountain tops on the horizon, everyone cheered with utter joy, and excitement. Jessie had only heard this type of excitement at sporting events or at the end of beautiful, yet controversial, firework displays. Although none of those could even come close to comparing to this grand spectacle and as the sun faded behind the mountain, the climax of cheers was musical and unanimous. That moment was followed at once by everyone saying the same thing at the same time as a blessing sent out to the world and everyone in it. "God Bless You in all you do. May you have a wonderful night and an even better tomorrow. Amen." Then they all cheered and started to disassemble. Part of the Capricians started to head back toward the top of the hill. Others walked around the lake. Lights began to come on here and there throughout the whole area. Some were even visible beyond the trees. Jessie was not sure if those were distance house lights or lightening bugs or something altogether different. Whatever it was, it certainly appeared magical. Jessie noticed that about half of the people were now spreading out blankets and seemed to be getting ready for something else.

"You are going to love this.!" Sarah said to Jessie with childlike excitement in her voice, taking Jessie's hand and leading her down the steps toward the field where so many were gathering. "This is my favorite part!"

Jessie could not imagine anything more spectacular than what they had just witnessed.

She followed Sarah down the steps over to a couple of Adirondack chairs that were sitting twenty or so feet from the gazebo. They sat down in the chairs, Sarah leaned back, looked up and let out a big sigh. Jessie followed suit, leaning back and then looking up. She could see stars starting to come out and lightening bugs flitting about here and there. But nothing spectacular seemed to be happening. In fact, that incredible sunset was fading quickly, and it was becoming quite dark.

Then Jessie heard Allion's voice near them and looked over to see him standing next to another chair. "Do you mind if I sit with you two. I want to be close by when you see this for the first time, Jessie."

Jessie looked up at him smiling and wondered why she could see the Capricians just as good at night as she could during the day. It was as if they had a sort of inner shimmering glow that could be seen just as clearly in the dark as in the daylight. She watched as Allion walked over to her, pulling His chair next to hers and sat down. Jessie realized she had not seen that chair sitting there before but thought maybe Allion brought it with Him. He looked at them both, smiled, then leaned back in His own chair, and sighed almost identically to Sarah.

So, Jessie leaned back again in her own chair and looked up. Then she started to get another one of those weird sensations like she did when the hole first appeared in that image of her sweatshirt earlier today. She felt as though something incredible was about to happen right before her eyes, but she had no idea what it was. How could anything top that sunset she just saw. Darkness was coming on even quicker now and the sky became darker than she had ever seen before yet at the same time, the stars started to twinkle brighter and brighter in all that darkness.

Jessie had often wondered where the saying came from twinkle, twinkle little star. They always seemed to be a steady source of light to her with very little blinking, but she had no doubt these stars were twinkling. They truly looked like self-illuminating diamonds filling up the sky. The longer she laid there and watched, the more stars came out. She had never seen so many stars in her entire life. She had never even imagined so many could exist or be seen with the naked eye. It turned into a sea of sparkling diamonds above her.

These stars were not just randomly scattered across the sky either. Jessie had always heard of the Milky Way and even seen pictures of it but had never witnessed it herself. In fact, she was not sure that any human had ever seen it quite like this before. The Milky Way was like a river of stars glistening so brightly, it looked like a sort of celestial highway. Jessie was not sure what she believed about heaven exactly, but if there truly was a highway to heaven, this milky way could definitely be it.

Visually she was overwhelmed with the beauty of the sky above her when she suddenly realized there was an incredible audible orchestra going on as well. There must be a million frogs, crickets, birds, and who knows what else, all singing together in what sounded like perfect harmony. She could somehow feel the sound of it throughout her entire being. She was so overwhelmed with emotion and felt tears running down her face. Then she felt Allion reach out and put His hand on her arm. It was so overwhelming she felt herself burst into tears. It was as if this world was healing all the pain, all the hurt, all the stress, all the worry, all the quilt, everything she had carried with her all her life. It was all just washing away, and she felt such peace and joy fill her entire spirit. Nothing else in the world mattered except being right there at that very moment seeing firsthand this incredible miracle and being present with these people, all of whom seemed to be the embodiment of love and kindness all wrapped up in every Caprician there.

No one made a fuss at all or even really acknowledged that she had just had an outburst of emotion. The symphony must have drowned out the sound of it to anyone other than Sarah and Allion. The three of them continued to watch the stars for a long time, but for precisely how long, it was impossible to know. Nature's symphony was the only sounds they could hear, other than the occasional cheers when a shooting star would fly across the sky, which happened quite often. Jessie had never been particularly good at spotting shooting stars before, but these were impossible to miss. Jessie had seen so many tonight she had run out of wishes. Now every time one shot across the sky, she simply whispered under her breath, "Please don't let this ever end."

Jessie was not sure how much time had passed. It was as if time did not exist there for a little while. She could not tell if she had been sitting there for a few minutes or a few hours. At one point though, Sarah leaned over and whispered to Jessie. "I don't know about you, but I could sure go for another piece of that pumpkin pie we had at dinner. How about you?"

Suddenly, Jessie realized she was quite hungry again. She was very full, what seemed like moments ago, so they must have been out here watching the stars for quite a while.

She turned to look at Allion and realized he was gone. She had no idea when He had left but He was no longer sitting in the chair next to them. She looked back at Sarah and nodded. They both slowly got up and Jessie followed her lead as they headed off to wherever that pie was waiting for them. She thought she would have a challenging time walking in the dark, but suddenly realized that everything was quite bright. It was almost as if a full moon was lighting the ground from an open sky overhead. However, there was no moon out this night. All that light was coming from the stars. It was such an incredible experience. She had never experienced anything even close to this.

Sarah leaned close to Jessie and said, "Just wait until you see the aurora borealis thrown in there amongst the stars one night!"

She could not imagine anything being more spectacular than what she had just seen but at the same time believed anything was possible here.

Jessie followed Sarah up past the gazebo, back toward where the picnic tables were before. Then followed her over toward the edge of the woods a little to the north of where they were earlier. There she saw the outline of a beautiful log cabin. This house was apparently not visible to her where they were before. As she drew a little closer, she could see a soft light inside as if from a lamp or something.

When they reached the bottom of the steps, Sarah said, "Go ahead and have a seat. I will grab us a piece of pie."

Jessie looked on the porch and saw chairs lined up all the way across the front of it. She took a couple of steps, chose a chair, and sat down. As she looked out across the meadow, it was almost as if part of the stars had fallen. There were so many lightening bugs lighting up the field that it looked like a beautiful and perfectly choreographed orchestra of light dancing across every blade of grass, flower or tree that could be seen anywhere. It reminded Jessie of an experience she had about ten years ago when she had gone to see the synchronized fireflies back in her own world. At the time she had been mesmerized by that sight, but this was that experience on steroids!

Sarah appeared with two saucers of pie and ice cream. She handed a saucer to Jessie and said, "So what was your favorite part of the show?"

Jessie tried to speak but felt a lump in her throat. She knew that if she tried to speak at that moment, she would burst into tears again. Sarah just smiled at her knowingly and said, "Me too."

They both sat for a little while, ate their pie and ice cream as they watched more of the show going on in the valley below.

More Capricians must have been heading home for the evening, because softly lit cabins started to show up all along the edge of the meadow and into the woods. Pathways that lead off into the forest started to appear as well, as if lit by lanterns or solar lights or something.

As soon as Jessie finished her pie, Sarah asked Jessie, "Are you ready to turn in for the evening?

Your room is all ready for you. I am sure you will find everything you need in there."

"That is truly kind of you. Are you sure it is not putting you out at all?" Jessie had started to feel quite sleepy but was also afraid to go to sleep in case this all ended when she woke up.

"Not at all and no worries. It will all still be here in the morning. Get a good night's rest. We have so much to show you and tell you about tomorrow. Your journey here has just begun."

Sarah led her to a room just down a short hall and showed her where things were. It was a beautiful guest room, with what appeared to be a big comfortable bed in the middle of it. A beautiful, obviously handmade quilt was spread out on top of it. The whole room looked so inviting. There was a little bathroom off to the left and a huge picture window next to a sliding glass door that led out to the wrap around porch on the right.

"What a beautiful room." Jessie said as she looked around.

"Thanks. Check the dresser there for PJs and let me know if there is anything else you might need."

"Thank you again so much for having me and helping me navigate Caprice."

"You are very welcome, Jessie. Again, we are SO glad you are here. If you need anything at all, just let us know. Otherwise, we will see you in the morning."

Jessie went over and sat down on the edge of the bed, and it felt as though she had just sat down on a cloud of cotton. She had never felt anything so soft, warm, or inviting in her life. She leaned back feeling as though her entire being was engulfed in ultimate serenity. She let out a heavy sigh and thought to herself, "I am about to get the best night of sleep in my life." She closed her eyes and the world suddenly disappeared.

## NEW BEGINNINGS

Very faintly Jessie heard a light sound in the distance but was not sure if it was in her mind or in a dream or in this new reality where she found herself last evening. It sounded like voices and children laughing. She could hear birds singing as well. Then she started to sense there was light all around her. It felt like a soft glow that embraced her gently, like warm sunlight streaming in through a window. She slowly opened her eyes to find that was exactly what it was. She was enveloped in a pool of soft sunlight as she lay there on the bed, blanketed in a warmth that caressed her very soul. She thought she had just closed her eyes a moment ago, but apparently, she had been asleep for hours. The darkness was gone. Everything was light and there seemed to be activity going on all around her just outside of this room.

She closed her eyes, rubbed her face, opened her eyes again and stretched. She slowly sat up on the side of the bed and hesitated for a moment, in part because she did not really want this moment to end either. She looked around the room and saw fresh flowers sitting on the dresser, stacks of old books on a bookshelf near the door and a beautiful window that encompassed the whole rest of that wall. It was covered only with a light sheer curtain. This was the source of the light hitting the bed.

She stood up, walked over to this window, and pulled back the corner of the curtain to look outside.

She could see the lake in the distance, with a beautiful field full of wildflowers stretching out before it. Children were running and chasing each other all through the field. A small herd of deer were grazing lazily just off the porch to the left of the window and a rabbit hopped into view and started eating with the deer. "Wow!" Jessie thought to herself. Then she saw movement out of the right corner of her eye. She knew it was something large and quickly looked in that direction. She was shocked to see a large black bear walking in the clearing so close to the house. She was suddenly terrified as she could see it was headed straight toward some of the children.

Jessie screamed out, "Look out." She then gasped as she watched the bear look at her, turn to the side, and walk over to the edge of the porch right in front of the window where she stood. It looked in at her and then scanned the pans sitting on the edge of the porch. Obviously, Gracie or Sarah one, had put leftovers in them because the bear started eating something and seemed quite pleased. Jessie just stood there with her mouth open because she had never seen a wild bear this close before.

More movement caught her eye and she saw two little girls running up closer to the house. She looked back at the bear and started to get nervous again. It is one thing for a bear to stand and eat some pie out of a plate, but it is another thing altogether for small children to run up to it. Jessie felt her heart go into panic mode. Then she saw Sarah step out on the porch and yell for the girls to hurry and come get breakfast. She did not even seem to notice there was a huge bear standing right next to the porch, but it was right there in plain sight. How could she not see it, she wondered.

The little girls came running up to the porch, looking over at the bear, and echoed a resounding "Hello Charlie" as they ran on into the house.

Jessie felt as if she could hardly breathe. She stood there for a moment and let her heartbeat slow back down. She turned and walked to the bedroom door and opened it. When she did, she could see Sarah down the hall in the kitchen scuffling about putting dishes all around the table. There was more food scattered about than Jessie had ever seen before at any breakfast gathering. All kinds of fruit, toast, some sort of quiche, a whole pan of biscuits, delicious looking gravy, and the largest plate of bacon she had ever seen. That might be a problem for her this morning. She quickly got dressed, ran to the bathroom so she could wash up, then walked down the hall mesmerized once again by the sight and smell of all this wonderful food.

"Good morning, Jessie, care for a cup of coffee or tea?" Sarah asked as she pointed toward a carafe and a mug tower at the end of the countertop.

"Yes, I would love coffee. Thank you."

As Jessie reached for a mug, Sarah continued, "There are sweeteners and cream right here if you would like either. Everything is 100% natural. The coffee beans are grown in the field behind the back woods, the sweeteners come from a variety of sources, all fresh and grown nearby. There is honey, maple syrup, and pure sugar straight from sugar cane that I grew myself. There is plain, hazelnut and pumpkin spice creamers as well, and some cashew milk that I just made yesterday, all completely dairy free by the way. Help yourself. I think they are all great. I sure do love my coffee in the mornings."

"Awesome. Me too." Jessie proceeded to make herself the best cup of coffee she ever had.

"Wow." Jessie turned around and looked at the plate of bacon and shook her head.

Sarah saw her and said, "Go on. Have all the slices you want. I can promise it will be the best you will have ever had in your life."

Jessie smiled but hesitated. "I am really trying to be vegetarian."

"Oh, go on, trust me on this one. Try one slice. I promise you will not regret it at all."

Jessie still hesitated and Sarah leaned in close and said, "Its vegetarian."

"No way!"

"It is. I promise."

At that Jessie reached out and took a couple of slices. She put a piece in her mouth and the flavor exploded into the most delicious bacon flavor she had ever tried.

"Wow. You are right. I have never had bacon of any variety that tasted this good, and bacon was one of my all-time favorite foods."

"I am right there with you. I love the taste of it, at least this bacon. The thing that I love most about it is that no poor animal had to suffer so we could enjoy something this amazing."

"So honestly, this really is not real bacon? This is amazing. How could it not be real?"

"Oh, it is real. In fact, it is more real than what you were used to that comes from animals. This food comes from the earth itself and grows in abundance here. Bacon made from an animal was just a substitute in your world for this staple after everything went a little crazy there and the original plant became lost shortly after Eden."

"Wow! I would have never imagined bacon this good and especially not coming from an animal. I never thought I could love bacon even more than I already did. This is amazing and with zero guilt makes it even better. So, it comes from a plant?"

"Yes, it is a vegetable. I would be happy to show you. It grows wild here. It is similar to an eggplant, but the vegetable looks more like a carrot. You just harvest it, slice it, add the seasonings, bake it for about twenty-five minutes until it is nice and crispy then enjoy it to the last crumb."

"It is amazing. I could live off this stuff."

"Well enjoy and eat all you want. There are three more full plates of it ready in the oven!" Jessie smiled and took a few more pieces from the plate.

At that moment, Gracie came bouncing into the room. "Good morning, Jessie, this is my friend Katie."

"Hi Katie."

"Hi, Jessie," Katie said smiling and waving at her, as she and Gracie each pulled out a chair each at the end of the table. They both sat down with a look of excitement on their faces as they looked around at all the food on the table.

Jessie smiled and then turned her attention back to Sarah. "May I help with anything?"

"Nope, we are all good and everything is about ready. Grab a seat and let's enjoy some breakfast. We have a big day ahead of us."

They all sat down, paused for a moment of gratitude, and began eating breakfast. Everything tasted so fresh and amazingly delicious, Jessie was blown away. Sarah went around the table and explained where each thing came from. The jelly came from blueberries growing on the north hillside. The biscuits were made from flour ground by her older brother from wheat he had grown and harvested last fall. She was so proud of him. She might as well have been telling a story of him winning a Pulitzer Prize. It was so heartwarming to see such a display of pure happiness.

Jessie did not think she had ever enjoyed any meal in her entire life quite as much as that one. The food was delicious, the laughter infectious, the happiness and peace almost overwhelming. Here Jessie was once again, in another moment she hoped would never end.

After that wonderful breakfast, which once again, Jessie had no idea the amount of time that had elapsed, everyone stood up to go begin their day. As they did so, each person picked up their own dishes, took them to the sink, washed them, put them in the drainer, thanked Sarah for a wonderful breakfast and went off to do their own things.

Jessie was about to follow suit and wash her plate, but Sarah took the dish from her hand. "I got this. I think Allion is waiting for you down by the creek."

"Oh okay. I didn't know that. I hope I have not kept Him long. But I hate to not help with the dishes or something though."

"It is perfectly fine. I absolutely appreciate the offer and sentiment. You are our guest here though. We would not think of it. Go on out and meet Allion. This is going to be a wonderful day."

"Okay, well thank you. I do have one question though. Where is the creek from here?"

They both laughed and walked over to the door of the cabin. Sarah pointed down the hill to the edge of the woods. "Go down to the edge of the meadow there and you will see it. It is just up the hill a little bit from the lake behind those trees there. Enjoy your day."

"Thank you. You too." Jessie said as she stepped out onto the porch. The sunlight felt like a warm splash of freshness on her face while a cool breeze blew up from the lake below. Even though she could not see it, she could smell honeysuckle faintly blowing on the wind. She took a deep breath, smiled, then walked down the steps and headed in the direction of the creek.

Each Caprician she met along the path acknowledged her by name and wished her a good day. She thought to herself that these were the friendliest, nicest people she had ever been around. She was even starting to get used to the fact that they all knew exactly who she was.

As she turned the corner on the path leading around the edge of the forest, she saw Allion sitting on a park bench down by a beautiful little rippling branch. She walked over to Him. He looked up and smiled as He patted the seat next to Him.

She smiled and sat down. "Good morning. I hope I didn't keep you waiting too long."

"Good morning, Jessie. No, not at all. I trust you slept well?"

"I did. Well, I guess I did. I do not remember it at all. I laid down on the bed, closed my eyes for just a moment and the next thing I knew it was morning and I felt perfectly rested, the most rested I think I have ever felt, so apparently, I did."

He smiled, "I am glad to hear that, Jessie. He leaned forward as though looking at something in the creek, then leaned back and looked at Jessie again. "So, now that you have spent a bit more time here, what do you think of Caprice?"

"This is the most amazing place I could ever imagine. It is so beautiful in every respect and the people are so nice. I feel so good being here. I have never felt so much peace in my life." Jessie felt like she could not even come close to expressing how deeply she already loved this place or how she felt being here. But in her heart, she felt as though Allion already knew.

"Do you not normally feel much peace?"

"No, hardly ever and never anything like the peace I feel here. Even the peace that I do feel back home is nothing like this and even that does not last long."

"Why is that?"

"There is just too much going on in the world and in my life."

"Talk to me about it."

"I am sure you do not want to be bothered with all my complaints."

"That is exactly what I want to talk to you about. That is why I came to meet you this morning. I want to hear all about your life and what brought you here."

"I have no idea what brought me here. I am glad I came, but still do not even know for sure how it happened."

"We are all still extremely glad you found your way here. So, tell me about your life back in your world."

"Well, it is difficult. Life in general is difficult. I am not sure where I should start. I mean it is not horrible and there are plenty of people in my world that have it a lot worse than I do. It just seems like the entire world is coming apart at the seams like I said before and I think being here and seeing what it could be like makes the contrast even more glaring."

"How about if you start with the first thing that you feel started to take your own peace away."

"Well, that would probably be when my parents died when I was a young child, 9 years old to be exact. We were all in a car accident. They were killed and I was injured quite severely. In fact, for a while there, they did not know for sure if I was going to live or not. But obviously I did. I pulled through and other than occasional arthritis pain, I am okay today as far as the accident goes.'

"What did you do after your parents died?"

"I went to live with my grandparents."

"How did that go?"

"It went the best it could I suppose. Both of my grandparents had issues and looking back at it all, their taking on a young child, I am sure did not help matters, but we all did the best we could."

"What were their issues?"

"My grandmother had dementia, so my grandfather had to take care of her and then after his son and daughter-in-law died, aka my parents, he had to take care of me as well. He had a couple of major health issues himself, so it was a difficult life for him, more so than anyone, I am sure."

"How do you think your living with them changed their life?"

"Before all of that happened, he was the deacon at the church where my parents and I had attended until the year before. Even after the other stuff happened that I told you about yesterday, he continued being a deacon there until my parents were killed. Afterwards, he switched to a different although similar church, but things were never quite the same. I am not sure my living there changed a lot in the trajectory of their life, other than the whole church thing. I think once I came to live with them and he switched churches, I think that might have changed him some, but I am not sure. I was quite young, and we did not talk about it much. I did try to be the least amount of trouble possible and helped around the house and with Grandmother all I could. However, that by itself, might have made it more of an option for him to turn to drinking like he did. Other than those things, I am not sure."

"Did all of that have a lasting effect on you and how your life turned out?"

"I am not sure. I mean I am sure it did somehow, but I do not remember the accident at all. Not really. Sometimes I think I do, but other times I think those memories are just planted in there by all the stories I have been told."

Jessie glanced over at Allion to see if he was reacting to her story so far. He was simply gazing off at the creek and seemed to be listening quite intently to her story.

He sensed her hesitation to continue and added," So, I am guessing there was not a lot of peace during that time?"

"Not really. There were good days and bad days. With my grandmother's dementia, most of the time she did not even know who I was. There were times she did not even know who my grandfather was. So that was a bit stressful for everyone, including her and especially for my grandfather. He did the best he could taking care of both of us."

Jessie got lost in her own thoughts for a few minutes before deciding to continue. "Then when I was in my early teens, my grandmother died and shortly after that my grandfather started having memory issues of his own. I wasn't sure if it was losing his wife after everything else or the drinking or something else entirely, Either way, I was afraid to tell anyone how bad it started getting, because I thought they might take him or me or both of us away and I felt like we were all we had and needed to stick together. We did what we needed to do through most of my teenage years until I was a senior in high school. Then he started to have other health problems. He was in and out of the hospital a lot that year and then died just before I graduated."

I stayed in the area for a couple of years afterwards. I earned an associate degree at the local community college but really had no idea which direction I wanted to go with my life."

"At that point, I had no reason to stay in the area, so I packed up my most important belongings and started traveling around the country, which I really enjoyed, but also felt quite lost a lot, both figuratively and literally. We did not have phones with built in GPS back then like we do now."

They both laughed. Then Allion encouraged Jessie to continue. "How did you wind up going back to your hometown?"

"Well, during the next 10 – 12 years or so after I left, I wondered around to different areas doing different jobs, mostly to pay for different classes I was taking along the way."

"What kind of classes?"

I took a lot of bible, religious and theology classes. As I said before, I had a lot of issues with the whole God thing growing up and a lot of questions but was always discouraged from "questioning God." Once I figured out for myself that it was not so much God, I was questioning but rather religion, it became a lot clearer what I needed to do. I decided in the end to take some classes to learn as much as I could about it all of it. I also wanted to learn to read the scriptures in the original languages of the bible, including Greek, Hebrew, and Aramaic. I figured that way I could learn more from the original texts without having to depend on all the different translations. It helped me to understand religions so much better and it helped me figure out a lot about God. I would not trade those years for anything. However, even that was a struggle, for myself and for my instructors along the way."

"What do you mean?"

"I absolutely loved learning about scriptures and the life of Jesus and how the earth came into existence, what God's purpose for the earth was and all of that. I just did not do as well with some of the other classes. In order to get a degree, I was pushed hard to at least pick a denomination that I wanted to be involved in after graduation, but I refused. I had no intention whatsoever of being a minister or otherwise. I just needed answers for myself. I was paying for the classes myself one at a time and felt like that was all I needed to commit to at that time. Many of my instructors disagreed and so even that was a struggle in a lot of ways. But still I loved those years and the education that I received. Once I learned all I felt like I could learn from the classes available to me, I left, closer to God, but even more removed from religion."

"That is all very interesting. Sounds like you really stuck to your guns on your primary purpose for taking all those classes. How did that work out for you?"

"It worked out about like I expected. I learned a lot more about God and the bible but continued to appreciate religion even less in most cases. I considered a career path in that field at one point but never really found any church that I could go to for any length of time without running into some kind of conflict within myself. So, I ended up following a more secular career path. I have always had a soft spot for children, especially underprivileged ones. So that eventually led me into the job that I have now.

"So, does that have anything to do with how you wound up back in the same area where you grew up somehow?"

"Yes, it does. A little while into choosing that career path, I got a job offer to be a child advocate in the local school system back in the next small town over from where I grew up. It was an opportunity that I could not refuse. It was better money than I had been making previously and there was the promise that I could make more changes in the children's lives there than where I was before. I was also told that all the foster places were better Christian homes and just an all-around much better situation for me and more importantly the kids. It all turned out to be slightly true, but not nearly as much so as I had hoped. I am able to help some kids at least somewhat, that are, for one reason or another, removed from their biological families. I try to help them have a better chance at a good life. Most of the time though, I feel so buried in red tape that I do not feel like I can accomplish as much as I would like to with these children." She thought about all of that for a moment longer and then continued, "But anyway, so that is how I ended up here where I am now. Well not here, here, but you know what I mean."

"How does it feel being back so close to where you grew up?"

"Better than I thought it would. I always loved the area. I just had a lot of difficult memories there as well. I have been back there about eight or ten years now. I have tried to reconnect a little bit with my family, but it has been slow going with everything happening in the world. My cousin Cody and I got back in touch shortly after I moved back. She is always trying to get me to go to this family gathering or that one. I have gone to a few of her smaller dinner parties during that time and went to the family reunion the year before the pandemic and then this year. That is where I was, when, well whatever this is happened." Jessie looked around as if once again trying to figure out where she was.

"We are extremely glad you did all that and found your way here. So, what do you think is the biggest issue you face in your life right now, that causes you the most stress?"

"Well, I definitely still struggle with the whole God issue, especially looking around at all the terrible things happening in my world right now."

"Tell me a bit more about that."

"Well as I said, I grew up in a church that talked a lot about hell and all the ways you could get sent there, but I never really heard much about an alternate option. Sometimes during the songs, I would hear about heaven or God's kingdom. I always wondered more about those options. But it seemed that if we were not singing about the afterlife, then the topic was not usually very nice. It always seemed like everyone was always so afraid of God and his wrath, that it never really made a lot of sense to me. I loved the idea of God's Kingdom and of a grand, wonderful, loving creator. I just often felt like I might have been the only person that wanted that specifically. Then looking around at all the things going on in my world right now, it just felt sometimes like maybe God is not so loving and kind after all." After a moment of speculation, she continued, "I really do not believe that. I definitely do not want to believe that. In the world that we are living in today, we need to know we have a good, kind, and gracious God on our side, especially in the midst of all the turmoil and ongoing disasters, even if we did, one way or another, bring them on ourselves. People also need to know there are still some good things in the world that must have come from God, at least in the beginning."

"Well tell me about that. What are some of your other beliefs along those lines and how did you come about them?"

"I always thought a lot about Jesus as well and figured there must be a lot of love in God's heart, especially if He were willing to sacrifice His only Son to atone for our sins. God must think good of us in some ways and if Jesus was willing to come and die for our sins, He must really love humans as well. I mean we did talk about that some in church of course, but mostly sung about it. We did talk about it a bit deeper in some of the classes I took. I also thought that God went to a lot of trouble to create such a beautiful place for us to live. Why would He do all that if He were just going to let us live for a few years until we died and then send the majority of us to hell. It just does not make sense and I have always wanted to know more, even as a small kid."

"As a child, how did you go about trying to learn more? What gave you the strength to stand up to your church and share those beliefs you did that day?"

I grew up in the country and spent a lot of time outdoors. Every time I would look out over a mountain range or see a beautiful sunset or spend time at the ocean on vacation and watch the waves of the ocean roll in, I could feel God there with me. I knew, absolutely knew, there had to be more to it than what I had heard about so far."

After a short pause, Jessie continued, "Even after I finished taking all those classes, I kept studying the scriptures and learning as much as I could about the entire bible and everything surrounding it. I know there does need to be knowledge of justice, consequences, and such, but there definitely needs to be more information out there about all of it, especially the hope. There must be hope, hope of a higher power that can offer us happiness, peace, security, and love. I really wanted to learn more about that part of God and His kingdom, then share some of that with others. That is a huge part of why I went into the field that I did. I really thought I could use some of that knowledge, hope and understanding I had gained to help others, especially children that felt a little lost like I had been." She paused, looking down at the ground.

After a couple of minutes and Allion had not said anything, she said, "I thought I would at least be able to help some kids that might be dealing with a difficult childhood or personal tragedy along the way. I thought that is what my job was going to be all about. But like I said, turns out it is mostly about shuffling through red tape all day long and I hate it."

"It sounds like you have had a lot to deal with but have tried to look for the good in life when you could. It even sounds like you tried to look toward God to help you through some of it. What are some of the good things in your life now?"

"I do have some wonderful friends and family. I especially love my cousin Cody. As I said, occasionally, I can help a child here and there at work too. I also love those rare moments when I can get out in nature and reconnect with God in some way and with myself."

They both smiled at that thought.

"I have told you all about my life. Tell me about Caprice and the creator of it. Everyone here seems so happy and at peace. There does not seem to be any worry about crime, pollution, or disease. What is the secret here?"

"Are you sure you are ready and really want to know?" Allion asked carefully, watching Jessie closely.

"Yes, I am absolutely sure. This place seems so perfect, peaceful, calm, accepting and has a very spiritual energy about it. I really want to know what the deal is."

"Well, in that case, I have a little confession of my own for you Jessie. I might as well get it out of the way now."

"I am listening." Jessie said hesitantly.

"Here in Caprice, you might say I am the Great I AM."

"Wait, what? So, are you saying that you are the God of Caprice?" Jessie said with a wide-eyed look of shock and disbelief.

"Yes, and I am so very glad you came to visit here and are allowing us this time to get to know each other."

"Well, you definitely don't seem like the God I was always told about in my world and besides if you were the God in my world and we made eye contact, I would spontaneously combust or something of the sort." For some reason, saying that aloud made her laugh. She tried to stop herself but then Allion burst out laughing with her and there was no stopping them for a moment.

Once He composed himself again, He followed with a very sincere sounding reply. "Well, you do not have to worry about that here in Caprice Jessie. I assure you. We can talk all day long and you will not get even a single puff of smoke coming out either ear!"

They both laughed quite hard at that one. As if this place was not surreal enough, it just took a whole other turn toward left field.

"So how does that work? I mean you walk around here with all the other Capricians as if you were just one of them. All this time, I thought you were just one of them. How can that work if you are their God? Do they know you are their God?"

"Yes, they do. The thing is, I do not really spend a lot of time thinking about the fact that I am their God. I spend my time thinking of them as my children." Jessie looked at Him, realizing she had tears in her eyes but was not sure why.

He continued, "The moment you walked through that portal, I felt the same way about you Jessie. I think of you as one of my children here as well. Again, I am just so very glad you came to visit us."

"I will admit, I am glad I came for this visit too. I am still not sure how all that happened or if I am even actually here, but whatever it is, I am glad I am getting to experience it."

Jessie thought for a moment and looked away from Allion and out across the field. "I wish things were less complicated where I came from and that I could find a God like you in my world. I would be happy with just some of this peace of mind back home that I feel here."

"I will make you a deal Jessie. As long as you are here, why don't you let me take on that role for you? You can get the feel of what it is like to live in a kingdom such as this and have the experience of a genuinely loving God who is your friend, as I hope you know I am. Maybe one day you will have it in your own world as well. While we are at it, I can help you overcome some of those issues that you have had to deal with for so long. Would you like that?"

"That would be nice. I am sure, as the God of Caprice, you have more insight than anyone else I have ever talked to before and you sure run a great world here full of happy people and the animals! Oh my God! Oops, I meant goodness." He laughed and then so did she, albeit a little nervously.

"Yes, the animals here are amazing! They are how they have always been, exactly as they were always supposed to be. I do hope you will get to spend some time with them and get to know some more personally while you are here. It is a gift beyond measure every day. I think Charlie, the bear has taken quite the liking to you as well."

"Oh, I would absolutely love that. That would be a dream come true."

"So, will you trust me to help you overcome some of these struggles you are having, maybe even help you find a way to make your world a better place?" He asked very gently and lovingly much like a dream father or grandfather might do.

"Okay, why not. I am not sure how long I am going to be here. You probably know that better than I do, but until I wake up or whatever happens, sure, let's do this. I need all the help I can get."

## LET THE HEALING BEGIN

Allion looked just past Jessie as if someone were standing behind her. Jessie turned around to see Sarah walking toward them with two glasses in hand. Jessie smiled and hoped they were filled with more of that delicious lemonade she had yesterday.

"I thought you two might be thirsty."

"Thank you. I am." Jessie took the glass and took a big sip of it right away. Allion took a much smaller sip of His and gently pointed toward the other bench sitting directly across from this one, that somehow Jessie had not noticed before.

"Thank you," Sarah said as she sat down and looked across the path at Jessie. "So how is it going today?"

Jessie looked away from her toward Allion and then back to Sarah. "Well, I imagine you know it's a little trying today."

"It could be a lot worse." She said and winked at Jessie knowingly.

"Do you feel comfortable talking with Sarah about all of this for a little while? I have somewhere I need to be for a little bit."

"Sure."

Both Sarah and Jessie watched as Allion stood up, looked toward the lake, and took a couple of steps down the path in that direction. Jessie glanced back over at Sarah, then back to Allion but he was gone. She looked back at Sarah and shook her head.

Sarah knowingly laughed out loud and said, "It takes a bit of getting used to, doesn't it?"

Jessie nodded in agreement and said, "So. Allion is the God here, eh?"

Sarah laughed. "Yep, that takes a bit of getting used to as well, doesn't it?"

They both laughed, took a sip of their lemonade, even though Jessie was sure Sarah only brought two glasses up with her and Allion had taken his with him.

"So, would you care to share with me a bit of what you were talking to Allion about?"

"I was just telling him that my entire world seems out of control, especially in stark contrast with life here in Caprice. I think being here is making that even more evident by the moment."

"Well, if it is any consolation, that is exactly why you came here. So that we can help you to get it under control."

"I cannot get my own life under control, much less the world."

"I promise there are things that we can do to help you find true happiness as you begin to see the world in a whole different light and in the end to help your world become a much better place overall. Ripple effect and all that. I will help you do that while you are here in Caprice, all of us will. Worst case scenario, if you decide not to follow through with it or go through the process or accept any of our help, you can have our full misery back guarantee." Sarah laughed aloud at her own joke then continued, "You can choose to go back to your world at any time and be just as miserable as you were before. Or you can choose to walk through these steps and find more meaning, more happiness, more hope, and more understanding, than you ever thought imaginable. That will be the catalyst that will help make your entire world a better place."

"You sure make it sound like a no brainer of a choice." They both chuckled.

Jessie thought for a moment and then said, "So, what does moving forward look like? What would we need to do first?"

"We have already begun, obviously without you even realizing it."

"What do you mean? How have I already started?"

"It is not as complicated as a lot of people think. Most things in our life we can overcome by following just a few simple steps. You took your first steps when you decided to follow that inner curiosity of yours and walk through the doors to Caprice. That is when the process began. That was your first step." She smiled at Jessie.

"Without even realizing it, you came here and admitted that your current life was out of control. You have started to believe in this world here we call Caprice and so the concept of a better world has become possible for you. Now here you are talking to our God one on one and allowing Him to help you in your life no matter where you are, here or back in your own world. By just explaining to Him all the things that are wrong with your current life that you would like to change or make better, you have begun an internal process of change. I would say that is a huge start in the right direction!"

"Well, when you put it that way," she laughed and said, "maybe this will be easier than I thought."

"No one ever said the journey would be easy. In fact, if it is too easy, you are not doing it right."

"Sounds about parr for the course."

"So, are you ready to take the next step?"

"Whatever it takes. What do I have to lose, right?"

"Awesome. Start by telling me what you think the root cause is of most of your issues in life and in the world around you? At least we can start there. Just tell me the first thought or word that comes to mind."

Jessie thought for a moment feeling as though she might be getting ready to go down the metaphorical rabbit hole, as there were so many things that were holding her back, she was not sure if she could put her finger on just one. But then it hit her, there was only one major thing, in her case, that gave power to all the rest.

"Fear. I think that is a huge part of it all for me. Fear of rejection, fear of hell. Fear of failure. Fear of gaining more weight. Fear of never doing anything of importance with my life. Fear of never being that one special person to anyone else. Fear that I might be wrong about the God in my world having a good side. Fear of the world coming apart at the seams and me not being able to do a single thing about it. I could really go on and on. I still have a lot of fear even being here in Caprice."

"Fear is a huge factor in the lives of most people, at least the ones that find themselves coming here. I would wager to say that it is at the root of a lot of the misery in your world, as well. They say the love of money is at the root of all evil. I think there is a lot of evil out there that has very little to do with money at all. From my experience, fear is a much more influential factor in most humans' lives than not. Even people who love their life, often have that small voice inside that says they are bound to lose it all at some point."

"I definitely see it a lot, everywhere I look in the world around me back home."

"What do you think your life would look like if you could remove all fear from it or at least all the limiting fear from it?"

"I really have no idea. I would love to wake up in the morning and know that I was going to have a good day. I would love to be able to walk into a room full of people and know that I was not going to do anything to embarrass myself. I would love to know I was going to wake up in a world like this every day. The fear I feel seems to have subsided here, but just the thought of going back to my world, I can feel it all bubbling up inside of me."

"How do you think this fear has injured you in your own life or even other people?"

"It has certainly been a part of what has kept me from being close to my family or advancing in my career or going out on a limb for much of anything really. I like my little safety zone I have built around myself. My little life bubble I call it."

"It might be more appropriate to call it your Fear Bubble."

"Ouch. But you are absolutely correct. It just does not sound quite as nice that way, but more accurate I would agree."

"So how do you think your fear has hurt other people?"

This stopped Jessie in her tracks and made her think a little longer and harder. She wondered if her fear had in fact hurt anyone else. She tried to think back to any specific times that she felt guilty about hurting others because of it, but most of the time she only hurt herself. She took a moment and tried to think harder because she now had an unshakable feeling that she had without intention hurt others as well.

Suddenly Jessie looked up from the ground and surprisingly saw Sarah standing in front of her with a full pitcher of iced lemonade.

"Would you like another glass?"

Quite startled by her sudden appearance in front of her with a brand-new full pitcher, Jessie very hesitantly asked," How? How did you do that? Where did that pitcher come from? You were just sitting right there and now a moment later you are here in front of me with it? I do not understand. It sort of freaks me out a little bit. What is happening here?"

"Time works a little differently here in Caprice. It certainly takes some getting used to. I knew you needed a few minutes to think about who all you might have hurt with your fear, so I thought I would leave you to it for a bit. In the meantime, I ran back up to the house, made us another pitcher of lemonade, put an apple crumble in the oven for dessert later and walked back up here. So did you figure out anything while I was gone?"

Jessie shook her head but held out her glass for a refill and said thank you. Attempting to regroup, she began to recall some of the ways that she realized she had hurt others.

"It is hard to think about how I might have hurt others with my own fear and insecurities. Letting down those walls seems very scary and even quite dangerous in some ways."

"Again, no one ever said it would be easy, but it is extremely necessary if you want to significantly improve your life moving forward."

Jessie took a deep breath and began talking about different ways that her fear might have hurt others. "I know my fear has hurt Cody."

"Who is Cody and how has your fear hurt them?"

"She is my cousin, as well as my best friend. She also has a cool job as a photographer and travels all around the world taking photos for a bunch of different travel magazines and other clients. She always wants me to go with her, but I am just so intimidated by that thought. It is so much easier for me to just stay home in my own little life, I mean, Fear Bubble. I have hurt her feelings more than once by not being willing to go, especially after I have told her that I would try my best to go.

She has had to find others to go with her at the last moment on more occasions than I wish to say."

"Okay, Who else?"

"As odd as it sounds, I feel like I have hurt countless children that I might could have otherwise helped if I had not been too afraid to try."

"Fear definitely has a way of holding us back from reaching our primary goals in life. Who else?"

"I am sure I hurt my grandfather at different times along the way. I did not trust him in a lot of ways either. I knew he did not really want to have to take care of me but did out of a sense of duty after my parents died. He tried to push me to do a lot of different stuff in my life, but I was just too afraid. I did not really see it as that at the time. I was so angry because I felt like he was just trying to get rid of me or get me out of his house. I did not ask to be there either. I would have much rather still been at home with my parents all those years. Looking back on it though after he died, I realized that he was just trying to be a good parent and get me to do more and have a better life and work harder to achieve the goals that he knew I could reach if I tried hard enough. There have been a lot of times I wished I could go back and tell him I am sorry for my anger or distrust. I still feel bad about it but can now see where a lot of it was caused more so by my own fear than anything else."

"Fear will certainly make us act out in a lot of ways for sure. Sometimes it is hard to recognize because we mask it with so many other feelings. What about yourself Jessie? How else have you hurt yourself by allowing fear to dominate different situations?"

"Yeah, you certainly hit that nail on the head. Fear certainly does dominate a lot of things in my life." Jessie said as her mind drifted off to the parts of her life that she wished were different.

"Are you okay Jessie?"

"Yes, I was just thinking of all the ways I have hurt myself or hindered my life by letting fear stand in the way. I cannot even imagine what my life would be like if it were not for the amount of fear that I feel, pretty much daily." Jessie felt a flood of nausea pass through her as she thought of more parts of her life that were lost forever, due to these fears.

"I would have certainly gone a lot farther in my career if I weren't so afraid of failure, people, embarrassment, and who knows what else."

They both sat there in silence for a few minutes while Jessie continued to contemplate how wonderful her life could have been if fear had not been a factor.

"What else do you feel like has held you back or caused you significant issues in your life Jessie?"

"Probably the next biggest obstacle that I deal with is negativity. I really struggle with that one sometimes too."

"Another big stumbling block if we allow it to be so. In fact, I would put that one right up there at number 2 for a lot of people, in your world and beyond."

Jessie stopped for a moment as if contemplating what she should say next.

"So, I am not sure that negativity is the right word to use. Maybe it is more a feeling of hopelessness. I think overall I am a pretty positive person. I always try to look for the best side of things and even people. I am always trying to give them the benefit of the doubt."

"What do you think has made your life feel hopeless and in what way?"

"Before I answer that, there is something I need to explain."

"Okay, I am listening."

So, here in Caprice, things seem vastly different than they are in my world. The God in my world and even the world itself is vastly different."

"How so Jessie?"

"Well let's start with the whole God thing. In my world, we have a quite different God. It often seems as though He is very wrathful and angry. I want to believe He is a loving God and have my whole life. However, our world is so full of hatred, war, disease, violence, pollution, one negative thing after another and God is often hard to find in it all sometimes, most of the time actually. I do look and try to give God the benefit of the doubt as well, but sometimes it is harder than others, to say the least." She hesitated before going further but decided to go ahead and get it all out.

"Here in Caprice, you get to walk around, talk, sing, laugh and have lemonade with your God. God is just not available to us that way in my world."

"Have you ever tried to spend the afternoon with the God of your world?"

"I don't even know how I would go about doing that."

"Let's start at the beginning. In your heart, you do believe you have a God in your world?"

"I was definitely raised to believe that there was a God, and have always wanted to believe it and even that He was a loving, kind, caring God but the older I have gotten, the more I have felt as though, if we did have a God present in our world, He either didn't like us very much, which would be understandable after all we, as a species, have done, or that He just didn't take a personal interest in us, especially individually."

"So, does anyone in your family have a loving, close, relationship with God?"

"I really do not know and cannot speak for them. Well other than maybe my cousin Cody."

"How is she different?"

"I do not know. She is always talking about God as if He is her best friend and lives next door or something. It is kind of weird at times really."

They both laughed.

"I will make you a deal Jessie."

"How about if while you are here in Caprice, I loan you my God?"

"You mean Allion?"

"Yes. He has certainly taken a liking to you and what else do you have to do? I am sure He would absolutely love to continue getting to know you better and help you in any way He can. Since He has the inside track on the whole deity thing, maybe He could help you sort out some of your issues with your own God. If nothing else, I know Him well enough to know that He could help you with some of those issues you mentioned before that are holding you back in your life. In fact, I will help you anyway I can as well. What do you say? What have you got to lose?"

"You are right. I have nothing to lose and potentially a lot to gain!"

"So where do we go from here?"

"Just by you making the decision to let us help you with all these issues you are having in your life, means you are halfway there. Not only will you be able to improve your own life, but you will be able to help make your entire world a better place."

"Okay, I will have to take your word on that one. I do not see how me spending time in some fantasy world or wherever we are here, is going to change anyone else in the world out there. It might help me in some way. I could kind of see that, but not anyone else."

"It all starts with you. I am sure you have heard the serenity prayer before, right?"

"Yes, of course. We all learn that prayer early on in life it seems."

"Right, well we have a unique way of saying the prayer for serenity here. It goes 'God, Grant me the Serenity to accept the things I cannot change, which includes trying to force anyone else to do anything they do not freely wish to do themselves, the courage to change the things I can, which is me and my actions and by my actions, the world around me, and the wisdom to know the difference, along with the discernment about the things I can influence for the greater good."

"I feel like I would have a better chance at changing others in the world, than I would myself a good bit of the time. There are certainly plenty of times that I wish I could change other people, places, or things, but I have always been taught that I could only change my own life. However, I really have not been highly successful at doing that yet either." Jessie thought intently for a moment then looked at Sarah. "So, are you saying that our actions always change the world around us?"

"Not always in some big profound way, but I am saying that until you learn to control yourself and make the changes in your own life that you would like to make, the changes that will make you happier, healthier, more fulfilled, and more God sustained, you will never be able to truly effect positive change in the world around you and that is not to say that you are not already effecting change, just probably not the change you wish you were making."

"We have a saying in our world as well, it is a scientific statement that goes, for every action there is an equal and opposite reaction. Sounds like that applies here as well."

"Absolutely. I think the difference between here and in your world is that everyone here in Caprice knows that and takes it very seriously and acts accordingly and responsibly. I think a lot of people in your world do too, but certainly not all of them. Would you agree with that?"

Sarah gave Jessie a few moments to think about that one.

Jessie looked up a moment later or so she thought, to find Sarah standing before her with a brand-new pitcher of lemonade and a bowl of apple crumble.

Started Jessie looked up at Sarah. "You know that will always freak me out when you do that."

They both laughed as Sarah filled up Jessie's cup, handed her a plate and sat down beside her.

"What are you two giggling about?"

Jessie was even more startled as she turned around to see Allion suddenly only a few feet away from them.

They both burst out laughing again, even harder. Allion knowingly laughed with them this time.

Then Sarah turned to Jessie and said, "Well, I am going to leave you all to it. It is about dinner time, and I need to head home anyway. There is something special I want to make this evening." She then turned her attention to Allion. "Be sure and send her my way in plenty of time for dinner." She winked at Allion then smiled at Jessie.

Jessie returned the smile, then glanced over at Allion and back toward Sarah, but she was gone.

## CLIMBING OVER THE WALL

"Ay ya yah," she said and shook her head. Allion laughed now for just a moment, a laugh that obviously came straight from His heart, filled only with love.

"So, I hear you are ready to let me help you with some of the issues you have going on in your life and in your world."

"How did you know? Oh wait, never mind. How could I forget."

"Let's talk about all of these things going on in your world that you wish were different and how you can help to change them."

"I am not sure I can change anything in my world. As you probably know, I was just telling Sarah how hopeless I feel to do much of anything in my world. I especially do not feel like I can effect change in the world around me."

"I think I can help you there. I do already know a good bit about your world. Let us just say I have observed it on more than one occasion. I know there is a lot of hate, crime, disease, war, all those things that you hate. Do you blame God for those things? And you can be honest with me."

"I am sure you already know that I do sometimes. It just seems like God should have the power to be able to put a stop to it somehow."

"You mean like the power He had when He created the earth without any of it to start with?"

"Yes. I just feel sometimes like He could use that power to strip the world of all that evil and fighting if He would."

"You mean like He did with the flood?"

"Well, yes, there was that. I never thought of it that way."

"He ended entire areas where evil existed in concentration at other times, like Sodom and Gomorrah. In the end, He even sent His own Son to help bring a message of Good Will to humankind and try to turn things around, for at least some of them, so that the rest of the world might be able to see the difference between

Good and evil that way. But again, that did not turn out too well either did it?"

Jessie dropped her head and shook it.

"The hatred, greed, jealousy, envy, and all those things that are so prevalent in the heart of man are all things that He warned humankind against over and over. He even had them write that down so they would remember to put in the necessary work to avoid them. Other times He did things like rescuing Joseph from prison and showing those people how, with trust in God, along with forethought and a little advanced preparation, life could be a lot better for them. By making the effort to do so, they warded off famine throughout their entire land. That should have been a fitting example of what to do and what not to do as well. They wrote that one down too, by the way." Allion looked at Jessie and winked.

Jessie smiled back at Him but was feeling a bit hit in the face with all those things.

"I never really stopped to think about it all that way before." Jessie said more quietly than usual.

"It is easier to blame God or blame others, even when the facts point to each and every individual having a role to play and being accountable for their own actions. The sum really is greater than the parts, but each of those parts, however small, must take place as well. Each act will lead to a ripple effect of some sort. Those ripples will change everything in their path. From there, it will continue to flow out into the world. If enough people choose to do the right things, the entire world will begin to transform. All it takes is a few people spread out around the world making those better choices and being more accountable for the choices they do make. Even choosing not to take deliberate action is a choice within itself. Individuals must be accountable for their actions and inactions."

"Maybe that is where I have fallen short the most."

"Where is that, Jessie?"

"Maybe by my inaction on so many different things and at so many different points in my life, maybe that is where I have failed the most."

"That is where a LOT of people fail the most. At their very core, most people are good and have good intentions but just do not follow through on the things the little voice inside might be trying to tell them to do."

Jessie thought about it for a few minutes and then said, "That little voice inside is both hard and easy to ignore. It does just keep nagging ever so slightly most of the time about one thing or another, but it is also easy to just busy ourselves with other things and keep our mind occupied so that little voice gets drowned out by the all the noise."

"Yes, you are correct Jessie. Most people in your world really need to spend more time in silent prayer and meditation, listening more intently to that little voice inside. I can attest to the fact that if someone ignores that little voice long enough, it will get increasingly quiet, but if they listen to it, it will continue to grow and shine. That is why people ignore it sometimes. They often do not really want to do the first thing that their inner voice is telling them they should do. So, they ignore it, hoping it will go away. Even if they do what they feel they need to do, they are afraid that by opening the door to start with, who knows what else might come flying out. So, they just leave it all closed and stay busy and ignore it all as much as possible."

"I am definitely starting to see where our inactions are as defining in our life and the world around us as the actual actions we do take."

"That is a huge step in the right direction toward understanding what the true journey is all about."

## CHANGING THE FOCUS

"I would really like to be more proactive in my life and head it in a more positive way. Can you and will you help me with that Allion? Help me to understand what it is that I need to do to make my life and attitude more in line with God's Will and purpose? I know it is another world here and quite different from my own, but maybe if I can learn here, I can find some way to carry it over in my world if I ever have to go back there. Not that I really want to. I would rather just stay here."

"That is a choice that you will ultimately have to make for yourself, just like most choices in life. You just need to wait until the facts are on the table in front of you, but do not wait too long. When that little voice starts talking, the time to act is there."

"My little voice inside is telling me, there are still a lot more things I don't know, maybe even some big ones."

"If I may, I suggest you use as much time as you can while you are here to get to know, understand and experience all that Caprice has to offer. Taking time to think about all of that, and let it sink in, will help you more than anything. Are you willing to open your heart and mind to the realm of possibility here in Caprice?"

"Oh absolutely. This place seems incredible. I want to experience it all and learn all I can. Honestly, I am not sure how that will help anything in my world, but I am certainly willing to try it. What could it hurt?"

"Excellent, I am so glad to hear you say that. Now though, I think it must be getting closer to dinner time from the look on Charlie's face," Allion said as he looked over Jessie's shoulder. "He is ready for that 'something special' Sarah was talking about."

Sarah looked behind her and was quite startled to see a huge black bear standing just a few feet away from them licking its lips. Her heart raced and she gasped, but somehow now with more excitement than fear. "Oh, my!"

Charlie made his way a bit closer to Jessie and she could hear a low clicking and grunting sound.

Allion smiled even wider and said to Charlie. "I am right there with you buddy. I can smell it from here too." He turned to Jessie and said, I think he wants you to follow him back to Sarah's house."

Jessie very nervously said, "Okay."

Allion continued as if He did not notice the apprehension in her voice at all. "We will talk again soon. Enjoy your evening. Be sure to look out over the horizon tonight. There is going to be a special treat in the sky just for you."

"More special than last night?"

"There is always something special in the sky if you take time to really look."

Jessie turned to look at Charlie and then back at Allion, but he was gone.

A soft grunt and a few clicks from Charlie and then he was on his way meandering back down along the creek toward the lake and of course Sarah's house.

She started to follow a short distance behind. "Very nice to meet you, Charlie." She said, in part as simple courtesy and because she was quite sure no one else was in ear shot.

Suddenly, Charlie turned, looked at her, grunted again softly, clicked a couple of times, winked, yes winked, turned back around, and kept walking.

Jessie felt like her heart would jump out of her skin. This was the best moment of her life so far.

The whole journey back to Sarah's cabin only took a couple of moments or so it seemed and suddenly she was smelling something too, that was out of this world. "Well maybe not out of THIS world," she thought to herself and giggled softly.

Gracie saw them and came running from the porch. She ran up to Charlie and gave him a big hug, then turned him loose and ran to Jessie with arms outstretched. "May I?"

"Of course." Jessie said just as Gracie gave her the best hug she had ever had. Then Gracie grabbed her hand and pulled her toward the cabin. Her excitement was, as always, quite contagious.

Jessie, Gracie, and Charlie all reached the cabin at the same time, just as Sarah stepped out on the porch and began to ring a bell, a bell which Jessie had not noticed before. Sarah was smiling and seemed so excited. There were pumpkins lined up all along the porch and beautiful fallen leaves all over the lawn. Color covered all the trees, and the fields were covered with beautiful wildflowers. The air felt crisp and clean and just the right temperature for the perfect autumn day. Sarah ushered Jessie and Gracie in the door, then said, "I could use some help." She then turned and waved as if to others behind them. Jessie turned to look outside again and there now were people all over the meadow, in front of the cabin and hanging out at a few dozen more picnic tables than Jessie remembered being there as they came running up to the house.

"Are you having some kind of party?" Jessie asked Sarah.

"Oh yes, we all are!" she exclaimed with immense excitement in her voice. Sarah looked at Gracie and they both shouted out, "It's Autumn Jubilee!"

"I am not sure what that is, but it sounds good to me and smells even better! What can I do to help?"

"Just grab a pitcher of lemonade and one of those pumpkin pies and head out to one of the tables. You are in for a special treat."

The next few minutes were filled with a flurry of people, food, drinks, laughter, a song here and there and the most joyous event Jessie had ever attended. Finally, everyone filled their plates with amazing food of all different kinds from dishes that everyone seemed to have brought with them. Then they all found their favorite place to sit. Then slowly everything got quiet. Jessie looked around nervously not sure what was about to happen. Then suddenly she noticed Allion walking down the steps. She had not seen Him arrive, but He was certainly smiling ear to ear seeing all the people that had gathered around. Then the crowd erupted in cheers and a resounding, "Thank you!!"

Allion nodded, waved at everyone, and said, "Bless you all. Happy Autumn Jubilee! Now dig in!"

The laughter and excited chatter could be heard from all directions. That was like the most beautiful song Jessie had ever heard. She looked down at her plate and literally felt her mouth watering. Suddenly someone sitting next to her nudged her and said, "Girl, dig in and yes, it is okay to eat the pie first! My sister cooks the best pumpkin pie in existence! Oh, and I am Greg."

"Hi Greg. So, Sarah is your sister?"

"Yes, she is my sister and Gracie is my awesome niece. I operate the sawmill just over the ridge from where you met Allion today. I also run the gristmill that makes most of the flour in this area as well."

"Oh okay. Cool. I had some of her biscuits this morning and heard about you then. So, no need to introduce myself I suppose?"

They both laughed and Greg said, "We are so glad you are here." They both laughed even harder then. "I'm sure you are tired of hearing that by now."

"Never. It is sweet. So, thank you." She smiled at him and continued, "So, sawmill, eh? How does that work in such a place as this? There does not seem to be any pollution or, well, it is just all vastly different from my world."

"Yes, we certainly do things differently here. We practice only sustainable harvesting of timber. Everyone here gets to choose their dream house and then we each help in some way to build it for them. Then that is where they live for many years. If they choose to move later, we start the process over again. But we never waste material. If someone else wants to move into their old house they can, or we will make it a community home for travelers or visitors. There is always a small percentage of houses that are available in different areas when people decide they want to move. They always look at those first to see if there is a house like they want in that location. If not, we can modify one that is there or build them a new one. However, we do this with sustainability as a top priority. Using our resources responsibly there is always enough to accommodate everyone.

There are a lot of other kinds of materials that people like to use for their homes instead of, or in addition to, timber, so it works out perfectly. We grow just the right number of extra trees to keep up with the need in addition to the trees that fall due to natural causes, other than decay of course. We are always sure to leave enough trees to keep the air clean and fresh for us all as well. It is all about responsible sustainability here and Allion makes sure we have enough of everything we need."

"That is so amazing. Nothing like how it works in my world, well at least not in all of it. We do have some gorgeous areas in my world, but there is a lot of room for improvement as well. So, did you build Sarah's house?"

"Well, I supplied all the lumber and did help build it, but by no means did I do it on my own. We have some very skilled carpenters here and one incredibly special master carpenter you might meet while you are here."

Jessie started to ask him if He was referring to THAT master carpenter but before she could, he continued telling her about Sarah's house.

"I think she had that cabin visualized from the time she was about Gracie's age."

"That is awesome. Her house is absolutely gorgeous. I love it and the location is perfect overlooking the meadow and lake like that with the little creek running down there below it close enough to hear from the porch. It is simply perfect."

"She designed it herself. It turned out exactly how she had always wanted it, so that part came easy. The location though, is a different story. She traveled and looked and debated and could not decide where exactly she wanted to live. It took her a lot longer to decide where she wanted to live, than for us to actually build her house."

"Well, she definitely made the right choice in the end for sure."

"Yes, she did. It is perfect for her. You will have to come see my house sometime if you would like. It is up on top of that ridge behind the waterwheel. Everyone laughs because I run the sawmill, but my own house is almost completely glass. It is covered in windows everywhere. I just love being able to see out in all directions and it has such a magnificent view up there. There is some wood of course, around the windows, on the floors and even the ceilings, but yep, the local lumberjack guy lives in a glass house."

They both laughed aloud, Then Jessie said. "I would love to see it sometime. I am not sure where the waterwheel is either though, but it sounds lovely."

"Oh yes, Jessie, you need to see our waterwheel, it is so beautiful, and it also provides most of the electricity we use here in our area of Caprice, at least for the larger operations like the sawmill. Each home typically includes a solar panel or two, maybe a wind turbine depending on where it is and most of the homes also utilize some geothermal to help with temperature control and such. We get everything we need straight from God here without any middleman so to speak. There are no electric companies or anything of that sort. We have life service technicians that are always building new solar panels and other devices to convert bits of nature into free and clean electricity, Then, they share it with the rest of us. The solar panels and such are used to heat the water, run the lights and any other electrical systems the homeowner has. We do love our conveniences here but not at the expense of our environment. We get our water from the reservoir, or private rain catchment systems. Some people in certain areas around Caprice also have wells if the rainfall is not sufficient in their area to meet all their needs. Our aquifers and other water sources are clean here, so it is just a matter of what is readily available and most environmentally friendly in each area. Each home has its own water storage system that is gravity fed, so we have no water company either. It is all perfectly clean because we do not have pollution or anything like that here. However, each home does have a filtration system because, well, we do have birds and such." He smiled and Jessie caught what he meant.

"That is so amazing. That is NOT the case in our world. Utility bills are a huge expense that each household must deal with every month. I am so glad that is not a part of Caprice."

They continued to discuss some of those more in-depth for a little bit. Jessie had often thought about trying to find ways to be more self-sustaining in her own world but did not know where to start. Greg had some great ideas to get her headed in that direction. He kept saying it was all about taking even the smallest steps to make a huge difference. Jessie hoped she would remember some of these ideas when or if she went back to her world.

As their conversation died down a bit, a woman sitting across the table from Greg looked at Jessie and said, "Have you been over to the dome or community garden yet? Oh, and by the way, I am Erica Danielle, but most people just call me Danni, with an I."

"Hi Danni with an I. Very nice to meet you." They both laughed and Jessie continued. "And no, I haven't seen any of those but would love to."

"I would be glad to show you after we eat if you would like?"

"Yes, thank you. I would love it and I can walk off some of this pie."

"Oh, we all love Sarah's pie. Even Charlie and his family. That is his favorite food." She glanced down by the creek and there was Charlie the bear that had earlier led her back to Sarah's house. But he had a lot of friends with him this time. There were a couple more bears, several deer, a whole family of racoons and several foxes sitting around looking up toward the picnic tables.

"Oh my gosh, that is so awesome. I have never seen anything like that before coming here. Seriously, they are all just sitting there together waiting for some of that amazing food."

"Yes, they all come around together for special occasions. There are a few times each year that the whole meadow will be full of animals of all kinds. Those there are just a few of the ones that show up."

"I am just blown away by the animals here."

"Me too. I love them." Danni said.

The next hour or so was full of food, fun, laughter, and a pure unadulterated joy that Jessie had never known was possible. There were a few kids playing ball down in the field, running around barefooted and laughing at the top of their lungs. It was the most wonderful sound, especially in contrast to the children she usually dealt with in her own world, especially at work. The children here in Caprice all seemed so happy and full of life, joy, and kindness. There did not seem to be any bullying going on or any shy kids or any of that, just pure fun, and joy as it should be with kids. Jessie thought about how amazing it would be if all children could grow up in this kind of world.

More animals were gathering down by the creek as well. Each person that finished eating took their dishes down and put any leftovers into one of the trays. Then they took their empty trays to the washing station and rinsed off their plate and cup, then headed off in various directions.

Jessie was enjoying just watching everyone when suddenly Danni said, "Caprice to Jessie."

They both laughed and Jessie said, "I get lost in my thoughts watching how this world works. It is amazing here."

"I totally understand. Want to see some more of it?"

"Absolutely." Jessie looked down at her plate and realized she had eaten almost every bit of her food.

"Of course, we will go feed the animals first." Danni smiled at Jessie, knowing it was just as much of a thrill for Jessie as it was for herself.

"You guys have fun." Greg said they started to get up.

"Wanna come along?" Danni asked out of politeness.

"Not this time. It's Autumn Jubilee. I am going back for more pie!" They all got up. Greg headed toward the cabin. Danni and Jessie started walking toward the creek.

As they each dished out their extra food in the bowls, Jessie could not believe all the animals that were there. All kinds of birds, chipmunks, rabbits, squirrels of several different varieties, racoons, foxes, opossums, deer, and so many others, several of which Jessie had never seen before and a few animals she could not even quite identify. She could have stood there all day looking at the animals, but Danni was waiting on her and she wanted to see the other stuff as well.

Just as she turned to walk toward the washing station where Danni had just finished rinsing her plate, she heard something behind her. It sounded like a few different voices simultaneously said, "Thanks."

She turned around to see who was there. She did not see anyone standing there but several of the animals were glancing in her direction. She cut her eyes back toward Danni with a confused look on her face.

"Sometimes they are more polite than others. Sometimes they are too busy eating to think about saying thank you."

"So, I am not crazy?"

"Nope, not one little bit. Come on, I have lots to show you."

As soon as Jessie cleaned and added her plate to the rack, they both headed up through the field toward the edge of the trees. Jessie glanced back toward the meadow, and realized it had about half the number of picnic tables that it did moments ago. Jessie just looked back at the path and followed Danni up the hill without saying a word about it.

Jessie had never been quite this far up the mountain before. The view was incredible. The valley was the color of wildflowers. The lake was bigger than she thought. The beautiful hardwoods were in full color display and the snowcapped mountains in the far background were even more majestic than they appeared to be from the valley below. The view would almost take your breath.

"Beautiful, isn't it?" Danni asked with a look of awe on her face, even though Jessie knew she had seen this same view hundreds if not thousands of times.

"It is hard to take it all in just how beautiful it is. The air is so clean, the water so clear and the sky, I have never seen a sky as blue as this, nor as many distinct colors of wildflowers in a field before. It is just phenomenal. It is mind blowing to be honest."

"I can only imagine the contrast between this world and the one you came from. It is amazing enough on its own but to add that aspect to it, yes, I can see how it would be almost beyond comprehension."

"Exactly. I could sit right here for hours."

"There are days I do just that. But for now, come on, we are almost there. I cannot wait for you to see our garden, which is where I feel like all the magic happens." She laughed and took off running around the back corner edge of the woods they had been walking past.

As Jessie came to the corner, she realized that the field they had just walked through, opened into a huge clearing just around that corner. Before her lay the most beautiful garden area she had ever seen. Row after row of all kinds of different foods and right in the middle was this massive greenhouse dome.

"Wow! This looks like paradise. Oh my gosh, you are right, this is amazing. There is so much food."

Jessie looked around at the different beds and could see so many kinds of fruits, vegetables, herbs and more. The tomato plants were loaded down with all kinds of different tomatoes. There was squash, cucumbers, egg plants, corn and just every imaginable kind of food. More than Jessie had ever seen in one place in her life. And the pumpkin patch was gorgeous. Hay bales were set up in a beautiful maze and more kids running back and forth through it. They were having a ball. "There is enough food here to feed an army."

"We don't have armies here, so might as well just feed as many Capricians, human and animal, as live in this area."

"So, this is all of the food for Caprice, or I guess this area of it?"

"Not all of it. A lot of people grow some of their own stuff, like strawberries or blueberries or whatever, if they want something right outside their door. But there is more than enough to feed everyone in our area right here. There are lots of different areas of Caprice where people live but this is our little neck of the woods and yes, it is more than enough to feed everyone."

"So, what is in the greenhouse? Is that where you grow your seedlings?"

"We do grow seedlings in there as needed, but a lot of our plants spring back up each year on their own from the seeds that were dropped the year before. Caprice has its own internal seed saving and sharing program, so to speak. But we also grow a bunch of plants there that would not thrive as well in this climate. We have a lot of citrus trees and stuff like banana trees, chocolate and coffee bean trees, pineapples, goji berries, all kinds of stuff that would not normally grow well here. But we all love those as well, so it is nice to have this dome where we can grow whatever we want to eat there. We are all just incredibly careful not to bring in any other non-native plants that can damage our local ecological system. That is especially important to keep everything running properly here. We only do food items from other places and only in the greenhouse. Greg helped me build it a few years ago and I have been playing around in it ever since. It is my happy place. Come on and let me show you."

Jessie felt like a little kid running along behind her to the dome. She felt more alive than she had in years, maybe ever. She was born into a world with pollution and smog and all that goes along with that. Here it was nothing but flowers and grass and plants of all kinds and fruit trees and it was just such a dream. For the first time in a long time, Jessie felt a sudden rush of panic that maybe none of this was real.

"Are you okay? You are white as a sheet."

"I, I think I am okay. I, I just." She paused for a second and then continued. "Is all of this really real?"

"It is absolutely real. This world is just as real as yours is. We are just living a different truth here. This is what God intended the earth to be. This is what your world would be like had sin not entered into it. To so many, this is Eden realized in all its glory."

"So, this is a world without temptation?"

"Temptation is not always the undoing of something good. We all have a choice. Eve had a choice in the garden. She could have chosen to trust God instead of immediately giving in to a promise that someone else told her that she knew was against what God had told her to do. In our world she made the right choice. Others have made some wrong choices along the way here, but nothing as severe as going directly against something God has told us to do.

We all know that one bad choice often leads to other bad choices, and it gets worse and worse with each one. The worst choice that some of us make here is having that one more extra piece of pie. Even that can have some unpleasant consequences if we do it enough. The difference is that it really is minimal, and we know it going into it. We purposefully make that choice and never blame anyone else for it. We are all given freedom of choice and free will. We do with it what we choose, but there are always consequences for both good and bad choices. Always. Whether we see them right then nor not."

Jessie thought about that for a bit and wondered how everyone could be so responsible all the time. This had to be heaven.

"So how big is Caprice?" she asked.

"It is the same size as your earth. You have only seen one small part of it so far. This is the area of Caprice that is closest to where you were in your world when you came to visit us. If you lived in a different part of your world, when you visited Caprice, you would have entered the corresponding area here."

"So, do you all travel between locations?"

"Oh absolutely, we can go anywhere we want, anytime we want. We can go around the world if we want, we just find out when the next shuttle is going to where we wish to go."

"Shuttle?"

"Yes, everyone here has a job they do, although we do not call them jobs here, we call them life services. Some people build houses, some people run energy sources like Greg, you met at Jubilee. Some people preserve the food, some people travel to bring back other kinds of food and seeds from other places, some people garden, like yours truly, and other people run the shuttle services back and forth between the various places. Some people are explorers and just go about the planet learning more of its great secrets then coming back and sharing all they have learned with others. We pretty much have all the same types of careers here that you have in your world, if you just took out all the greed, money, power, politics, and all that. We all have gifts, skills we have been blessed with and things that we just absolutely enjoy doing the most and so that is what leads people here to follow their heart and pick their life service depending on what brings them and others the most joy. We all also make sure we still have time to do other things we enjoy and spend plenty of time with God and others and enjoying all that Caprice has to offer."

"That is incredible. So, when you say, no greed, money, power nor politics, do you mean that you do not have any of that here?"

"That is exactly what I mean. We have no need for any of that here."

"I just do not understand how a world could exist without some of those. Although at the same time, they do bring a lot of chaos along with them. I have heard my whole life that the love of money is the root of all evil, so I could certainly see how not having it could make the world a better place but how does it all work?"

"Maybe it would be better to ask you how it does work in your world. Say you have a bunch of money laying around on your table at home, what does it do or provide for you?"

"That would be nice. I would say it provides security first and foremost."

"So, it is like a weapon of some sort that you can use to do battle with someone coming against you?"

"No, not that type of security, at least not exactly. Money provides the knowledge that you will have whatever you need, food, housing, repairs, medical care, entertainment, stuff. Having money just means that you can do whatever you want, whenever you want and not have to worry about not having enough money to do it."

"So, the money itself only holds value relative to the things you can trade it for, not the money itself?"

"Exactly, unless you count rare money or coins that people collect."

"Don't most people in your world try to collect as much money as they can?"

"Yes, typically, but most people prefer to collect the stuff that you can buy with the money. However, some of the actual money is rarer than others. For example, a dollar bill that was misprinted or a coin with some sort of defect on it from the mint where it was made."

"So, some of your money is printed, do you mean like from paper and others are minted out of something else?"

"Yes. Paper money is printed out of a special type of paper and coins are made of various kinds of metal."

"What sort of metal?"

"It has varied over the years. Nickel, Copper, Zinc, silver and even gold. It changes over the years. As one metal becomes rarer or resources start to run low, they switch to another cheaper more common metal, until that one becomes rare and so on."

"So, does the metal money go up and down in value depending on what metal they are using and how available it is? Is the paper money less expensive because it is something they print on a more readily available material like paper?"

"Oddly enough, metal money, coins as we call them, are the ones that are valued the least in most cases. The paper money is worth whatever they print on it to be worth, relatively speaking to whatever is going on with the market."

"So, they just print it and say it is worth whatever they want it to be worth? Who gets to choose the amounts?"

"Some branch of the government, I am sure. They are supposed to have gold to back up however much they print and are only supposed to print enough to cover inflation and any old or damaged money they take out of circulation to the public. However, I am not real sure how it all works. I do not think most people really do. They just go about earning all of it they can to go buy things and do not really stop to think about it much beyond that."

"Even though you are not sure how it works, you and most people in your world, spend the majority of your time working for someone else to try to get all of it you can?"

"That about sums it up. But there is no other way to buy all the stuff we need, like cars, houses, utilities, food, clothing, all that. We must earn money to buy those things and the more we have, the better of those things we can buy. And now we also have digital currency in various forms."

"What in the world is that?"

"Digital currency is money that is not backed up by the federal reserve in any way but rather is as valuable as the creator says it is. So, people can take their cash and send it to the creator, or the company that the creator set up, and buy as much of the digital currency as they can afford with the regular currency they have earned. Supposedly, the more people that buy into it, the more valuable it becomes, until someone finds out that the money is not just sitting there waiting on everyone to share but was spent by the person creating it for their own needs or wants."

"Isn't that why they would create it?"

"I would think so. But it gets into a real mess when all that invested money is gone and there is nothing to back it up. That is where the problems come into play. That is a huge problem in our world too but for some reason, people just keep buying it all over and over, I guess expecting things to be different next time. Sometimes it is. Sometimes it is not. When it all first started, there were a bunch of people that made millions of dollars in cryptocurrency by creating these digital items that people could only purchase with cryptocurrencies and these items could, for the most part, only be used in virtual worlds. A lot of people made a lot of money doing that in a brief period of time. However, a lot more people did not make anything at all. Others lost everything they had. After a few failed companies involving some of these serious get rich quick schemes, people started to be a bit more cautious about it all. Eventually it became just another form of currency for us. It just happens to be one that you cannot see, touch, or hold in your hands. Who knows what will be next."

"So does everyone start out with a certain amount of money and then do with it what they want and use it to try to make more money eventually?"

"No, that is a game we call Monopoly. When you start out in life, you do not have any money or anything, unless you get it from your parents or someone. The parents are supposed to take care of you for the first few years of life. That is not always the case either, but they are supposed to do so. Once you reach a certain age, at least in most cases, you must start making your own money and figure it out from there."

"So, when do you get a house and all of the stuff you need to live a normal life on your own?"

"Whenever you can afford it or have good enough credit to buy it. That is what most people live on, credit."

"And what is that?"

"Basically, that is where a person gets a job and depending on how much money they are bringing in, different companies will loan them a certain amount of money that they can use to buy a house or car or whatever, and then they pay it back monthly with the money that they earn from their job. So, the people that have the most money all join together in the banking system and then the banks use that money to loan to people with less money to buy the things they need. Then those that borrowed the money must pay that amount back plus more to go with it. We call that interest. They just pay it back a month at a time over a few years."

"So, the people with the most money get more and more money and the people with less money, have to keep earning more and more money and giving it to the people that had the most money to start with and all so they can all have their necessities in life?"

"Pretty much."

"Oh no. That sounds like a scam or something."

"It does, doesn't it? It is a vicious cycle that most people where I am from get involved in quite early on in life. I mean if you get out of high school at 18, maybe go on to college if you are lucky for 2 to 4 years on average, which you also have to pay money for, then get a job and buy a house, for most people that means on credit of course, and do the average 30 year mortgage loan, you would be around 50 years old before you had it paid off, not to mention, all the other things that you might get on credit in the meantime, cars, phones, trips, additional education, and so on. Most people spend most of their time working to pay for credit used to buy things they are already using and are using it up before that item is even paid for, like with cars, etc. including houses. Those are the biggest things that most people buy. Most things bought on credit by the average person are worn out before they have them paid off, so then they must buy another one. Even if they can trade the first one in, it is not worth as much as the new one, so they still end up having to use more credit to buy the next one. Once they buy into the whole credit thing, it often becomes almost impossible to break out of."

"So, why don't people just help other people build houses or whatever it is that they need and not charge them for it and that way everyone gets a house for free, and no one ends up in debt or having to work so hard and always being behind the game?"

"Very few people do anything for free in my world and it is hard for them to do so, because even if they donated their time to build it, they would still have to buy all the materials."

"So, who sells them the materials? What if those people gave those away?"

"That would be the lumber companies or brick companies or whoever, depending on the materials used to build the houses, etc. They are not going to give those away because they must pay for the source supplies to make the lumber, etc."

"So, who do the lumber companies buy the supplies from? Who charges them for say the trees to make the lumber? Aren't those just kind of growing out of the earth like they are here."

"They are but they are the property of the landowners. Whoever worked out enough money to buy the land can do whatever they want with it. Landowners sometimes work with a timber company to come in and cut down the trees on their land and charge them for the timber. Then it goes up the line from there. Everyone makes some money off it as it goes along, eventually ending up with the homeowner paying the largest amount overall."

"So, what if the house buyer agreed to come plant trees for the landowner, then everyone else along the way could donate their time to help that person get the house they want. And each person could help the next person, so in the end, everyone would have a house, and no one would be in debt."

"Maybe in a perfect world, but that is not how it works back home. It is all about money, from beginning to end. Most people's entire life is all about getting the best job they can, to earn the most money they can, so they can get bigger and better things and still end up spending more than they have and often leave quite a bit of debt when they die."

They both stood in silence for a few minutes contemplating how that vicious cycle could ever work out for the greater good of everyone or the individual. No answers came to either of them, so Jessie continued, "Primarily in my world the rich people just keep getting richer and most everyone else spends their life trying to be as rich as they can be and still survive. How does it work here? I mean how do people advance and do the careers they do and why even do it if money does not exist?"

"People can go to advanced school here in Caprice as well, but it is to learn about something that they enjoy doing or feel called to do that will, in its own way, make the world a better place as well as their own."

"I can definitely see in the contrast from my world to Caprice, just how much the love of money is the root of all evil, but it would be impossible to navigate my world without it to some degree."

They both thought for a few minutes as they turned and began walking slowly around the garden.

Then Jessie continued, "I think a lot of the issues in our world stem from the way it is all set up to begin with. Our entire planet is divided into individual societies, nations, states and so on. Those are run by different political factions, all of which pretty much have the same motives. Their primary purpose is to make their nation as rich as possible and to have the biggest, and best of whatever they can have. There are only a few of those countries that are on top of the food chain though, so to speak, while other smaller countries are often just barely surviving, a lot of them without even enough food or shelter or other necessities for most of its citizens to live any quality of life. Money and power. Power and money. It all goes hand in hand. Greed in one causes more greed in the other. It is all such a devastating cycle. That is a big reason our world is in the mess it is in or at least a main contributor to it."

Danni shook her head and looked down at the ground as if trying to comprehend what Jessie was telling her.

Jessie sensed her confusion and pressed a bit further. "So, no money ever exchanges hands here in Caprice for anything?"

"We do not even have money or anything like it. Everyone contributes in their own way, and we all have something special to offer and one thing is just as valuable as the next. We have builders, gardeners, musicians, artists, writers, tour guides, scientists, and so much more. Everyone finds something they truly enjoy and do it for as long as they want and then they go do something else. Sometimes people do several different things at once. For example, I am a gardener myself but also love traveling around the world and learning different animal languages. Who knows what I might want to do next but for now, I love both of those so much I cannot imagine wanting to do anything else."

"Animal languages?" Jessie exclaimed. "That has got to be the coolest thing in the world!"

"Oh, it really is. I can speak over 1,000 different animal languages and have taught many of them to speak our language as well. It is such a fun endeavor, and everyone so enjoys getting to know the different animals and visa-versa."

"Wow. That just blows my mind. This really is the most amazing place imaginable."

"Your world started out the same way Jessie. Didn't the first people in your world talk to the animals?"

"Well, I suppose they did come to think of it. Adam named all the animals right at the beginning of it and a short while later, when the serpent began speaking to Eve trying to tempt her with the forbidden fruit, she was not shocked, nor even acknowledged that it was anything out of the ordinary when she heard it speak. So, yes, apparently talking to the animals was normal there in the beginning. Now that I think about it, walking around the garden while talking to God was a normal occurrence back then as well, according to our bible."

"Oh, that reminds me. Have you been over to talk to Allion yet today?"

"Yes, I had a long conversation with him just before Jubilee dinner."

"Oh, goodness. That was a few days ago. I did not mean to keep you this long. I am going to go and leave you to it for a little while."

"Wait. What do you mean, that was a few days ago?"

"Time, or the lack of that constraint, is a bit confusing here I know. But once you get used to it, it is quite incredible."

"Confusing would be one way to put it."

They both laughed and Erica Danielle started to walk away.

Jessie called after her, "Where I am supposed to meet Allion?"

"Here in the garden of course. He is always in the garden."

Jessie turned and glanced around the garden then back in Danni's direction, but she was gone.

Jessie decided to stroll through the incredible garden grounds for a bit and see if she ran into Allion when she suddenly heard his voice next to her.

## PRAYER AND MEDITATION

"It is so good to see you here today, Jessie. I am glad you have decided to stay with us all this time."

Suddenly Jessie's mind shot back to what felt like a couple of days ago, but she was quite unsure at this point how long it had been.

"I am still not sure how I am 'deciding' to stay or go, but I am not complaining. I absolutely love it here and if I have my way, I will stay here forever."

"That is something I have been wanting to talk to you about."

"How are you feeling about your old world, now that you have spent so much time here in Caprice?"

"Oh my gosh, I am not even sure how to put it into words. It has all been such a whirlwind. This place is so incredible while my world is seriously messed up and so far removed from anything like this at all."

"If you saw my world, Allion, I think you would be just as shocked as I am here seeing this one, but not in a good way."

She thought for a few minutes about her world and then continued. "I just keep thinking about it and how different it is. I know I have said it before, but the contrast is just so profound. My world is so full of greed, hate, crime, corruption, illness, envy, selfishness and so much more. It is nothing like here. Nothing at all." Her face dropped with sadness, and she felt her whole spirit take a hit just thinking about the world she came from.

"There are some good things in your world as well though right?"

"Yes, there is. There are a lot of good people there. It is unbelievably beautiful in so many places. We have all kinds of amazing animals there as well. So, yes, in some ways, it is very much like Caprice. I imagine it could have been a lot more like it if humankind had not gotten in the way."

"From my understanding, it was once just like this place in every way. Then you are right, it began to change. Temptation came into the world and humankind started making some very bad choices, one after another, with each one making the next bad choice even more imaginable and easier to carry out."

"That pretty much sums it up. From the very first human couple, things started to go bad. They were in a garden called Eden. All they had to do was live, apparently like the people here do, and everything would have been incredible. However, they chose greed, temptation and to not trust the God of our world. It all went downhill from there. But in my understanding, God had initially planned on humans spreading out, populating the entire earth, and turning the whole planet into a beautiful garden just like this one. Had they done that, I wonder if it could have wound up being like this place in every way."

"So, you believe that your world was supposed to be like Caprice?"

"Yes, I do think so. That is what God wanted it to be. Even in our most sacred texts at the beginning of time in our world, that is exactly what our creator told them to do." Jessie sighed in exasperation. "Had they only done it, our whole world and every living thing in it could be living the good life just like here."

"So, this God of your world, had a plan, but humans ruined it?"

"Yes, that is exactly what happened."

"Was it humans alone that ruined it?"

"Well, no, there was this angel that had turned bad and started a great contest with God, saying that he could turn humans away from God. He is the one that came down and spoke through a serpent to Eve and tempted her to eat a forbidden fruit that God had specifically told them not to eat. Satan, as he is called, lied to Eve, and told her that the fruit was okay to eat and would open their eyes and make her and Adam more God-like themselves. So, he tempted her to go against what God had told them to do and Eve made the decision to do so. She chose to disobey God and take part in this forbidden act so she could gain knowledge, and power. She allowed greed, self-righteousness, and temptation to rule her life and actions. Then she also tempted Adam with the same proposition. He followed suit. When they made those choices, that is when it all started to go terribly wrong. They chose to listen to this stranger and follow him rather than to trust their own loving creator that they knew well and had spent time getting to know. He had given them everything they needed and in such wonderful abundance. He was going to allow them to inhabit the entire earth and have everything they could ever want or need that was in line with His incredible creation. It was His after all. But they chose to go against Him and choose Satan's way instead of being grateful to this grand creator. They just threw Him to the curb. Of course that upset God immensely, so He kicked them out of His garden. He could have just ended their whole existence at that moment and been done with it. But He still loved them, and He wanted to give them another chance. Unfortunately, they had introduced sin into the world. That sin brought death and mortality along with it and it has gone downhill ever since." Jessie shook her head, rolled her eyes, and looked truly angry.

"That upsets you terribly doesn't it, Jessie?"

"Of course, it does. All they had to do was trust in God and be obedient in those simple rules that He gave them, and the entire course of humankind could have been different. We could have all been living in a beautiful paradise garden, just like the one here in Caprice. But instead, they had to get greedy and selfish and ruin it for everyone else, including themselves. When Satan tempted them to disobey God, he knew what would happen. That is why he did it. He wanted to turn them against God and get them to follow him instead. So, he lied to them about it all. However, all they had to do was trust God over this stranger. They could have lived forever in happiness and peace and had all the wonderful gifts that God had in store for them. But no, they had to go after their own greed and throw it all away. It does make me very mad. They ruined it for all of us."

"I understand your anger and frustration. So, do you feel like all hope is lost for your world, Jessie?"

"I do not know. It is hard to know. We are so far removed from anything resembling what the world was supposed to be. It would be hard to imagine it somehow turning around now. Although come to think of it, you did mention some good points earlier about how our God has tried to help give our world a good restart, especially with a great flood that we had there, but humankind still messed it up in the end. But I guess God could do it again if He wanted to and surely after all this time, we would get the message and do things differently."

"What do these sacred texts you speak of say about it?"

"Well, they say that a time will come when the world gets so bad, that God will have to step in and destroy all the wickedness like He did with the flood. When He did that, the flood waters covered the entire earth and destroyed most of the people on it, all but one faithful family. Well at least the father was faithful. There are some questions about the rest of the family. Eventually that family multiplied and filled the earth again. God promised never to destroy humanity by water like He did then. From my understanding, the next time, He will begin by reigning His wrath down on all of those who stand against and attack his chosen people, the Israelites and then He said He would make a new heaven and a new earth. While it does sound promising, I am not sure how it will all come about. But I do think that things in my world are at a turning point where He is going to have to do something. All the so-called prophesies have just about been fulfilled and more are being fulfilled every day. I do not feel like it will be long before our God brings His wrath against all those who oppose His people and are destroying His earth. I think at that point, He will destroy wickedness all around the world and put a stop to it once and for all. The scriptures say He will do all of that before humankind completely destroys the earth. There are days when I think He better hurry."

"I know wrath and destruction doesn't sound that good, but getting rid of all the wickedness would be a good thing, wouldn't it?"

"Yes, I just hate that it has come to that. I am not sure how much of the world would be left once that happened."

"By world, do you mean the earth itself or the people in it?"

"Both I suppose. I imagine a lot of people would be destroyed and there would have to be a lot of destruction on the earth itself as well. Although God could destroy all the people on the earth and do so without causing nearly the amount of damage that humas are causing the earth every day." She considered all of that for a moment and then continued. "Maybe the damage would be minimal to the earth itself and then God could just make the entire world new again, kind of like He did after the flood. Maybe that would be part of the whole new heaven and new earth prophesy that is mentioned several times in the bible."

After pausing for a few minutes again, she continued sarcastically, "If that is what He does, He might have to make the world this time without humans, because they sure messed it up each time before."

"Don't you think they might have learned their lesson like you said before?"

"It is hard to say. At times I do not think so. Otherwise, they would stop doing all the insane stuff they are doing. They would stop all the fighting, crime, and wars all over the planet. If they had learned their lesson, they would not do even a small portion of the stuff they do today. They are destroying the entire earth, humanity, and the animals, even right down to the very air they themselves are breathing. They do not know any other way to live at this point."

"What if suddenly, the way they are living came to a halt and that way no longer worked? Then they would have to find a different way to live. Do you think that would work?"

"I really do not know. There are days when I feel like humans would still find a way to mess it up again, even if they were placed back in the Garden of Eden."

"Is that what was foretold would happen this final time when God stepped in and took matters into His own hand?"

"No, it says that after God destroys those that came against His people, that there would be a lot of other changes on the earth, even in the form of the earth itself. It says that the entire world would indeed be made new again. It also talks about how the meek will inherit the earth and how those living on it, would turn their weapons into plow shears."

"Well, it sounds like they would have to learn a new way to live if all of that was the case." He glanced over at her and said, "It is hard to go to war with each other if your only weapon is a plow. What would they do, threaten to dig up each other's gardens?"

They both laughed and then Jessie said, "Well I guess first they would all have to start planting their own gardens so they had something to eat and that would keep them too busy to go trying to destroy other people's gardens. Who knows, they might even begin to have more compassion for each other, knowing they were all in the same boat at that point.

Jessie thought for a moment longer and replied. "That would probably be the only way they would change."

"What would it take for that to happen?"

"That would definitely take an act of God, without a doubt. Because no human on earth could accomplish that. Not at this point."

"Do you personally believe that your God has the power to do that? And that it might be His plan?"

Jessie paused and thought for a little while, unsure what she believed about that.

The sun suddenly began to set behind the horizon. It was so beautiful as Jessie and Allion sat and watched it for a few minutes. Jessie knew at that point that if she needed to head back to the cabin, Allion would make sure she got there safely. Then as suddenly as the sun went down, Jessie could feel it shining on her back and the world began lighting up again, as if at the same moment the sun went down in front of her to the west, it came up behind her in the east. She turned her head to look over at Allion and smiled. He smiled back at her. Had He not been sitting there; this experience would have been very disorienting. However, she felt as though it was a sort of gift to her from Allion. So, she just enjoyed it. This whole cycle happened several more times as she sat there and thought about what Allion had asked her.

Finally, she answered, "I do believe that if God has the power to do any of the things that have been told as part of our history, from creation forward, or any of the prophesies foretold that have already taken place or that are still supposed to happen, then I also must believe that He has the power to fulfill that original purpose as well. I know the new earth is one of those final prophesies that was foretold. So, in answer to your question, I do believe He has the power to do all those things, past, present, and future, that have been foretold including winning the battle against evil and being the ultimate victor on the earth that He created."

Jessie took a few more minutes, or days as the sun rises and sunsets would suggest and thought about this even deeper.

She finally turned to Allion and said, "What are your thoughts on it? I would think that you have some definitive insight on these types of things. Care to share?"

"I would definitely say that if one had the power to create the earth, and everything on it plus the entire universe surrounding it, as well as everything else in existence while doing so in a way that made it all fully self-sustaining, except for the part that humans have messed up, that He could also bring about His Purpose on His one favored planet. He would not be thwarted by some evil entity or any animal or even angels He created that turned against Him. I am betting that in His time, all will be turned into exactly the place He originally wanted it to be. He will win out over evil forces of any nature."

They both sat through a few more sunrises and sunsets. Then Allion continued, "Maybe that is why you came here to Caprice. Maybe your world is closer to that time of Him changing it all back to the way it was supposed to be than most people think."

"I definitely believe that time has just about come, but I am not sure what my coming here would have to do with it."

"Maybe you are supposed to carry the message back to them about how the world is supposed to be. Maybe experiencing this world gives you an insight that your world needs to hear about."

"Oh, I am not the person to share that information with the world. I am pretty much invisible there. No one outside my immediate circle knows me, I do not have any kind of social platform and I am very shy on top of it. I stick to myself, and I prefer it that way. There are a LOT of other people that have far more followers and could reach a lot more people than I ever could."

Allion placed His hand on hers to calm her down a bit. "We have a saying here that God does not call the qualified to do a job, He qualifies the called. I personally, as the creator of Caprice, can attest to that fact daily. Boy, do we start out with some doozies of unqualified apprentices in all kinds of fields." He shook his head but smiled and winked at Jessie.

They both laughed aloud. Then they looked out over the horizon as the sun seemed to slow its pace across the western sky.

"So, how does all this world work? I mean I get that money is not a consideration here. Which is mind blowing but starts to make sense if you take it completely out of existence and think about it for a bit. But what about the rest of it? What about leadership roles, governments, and all of that?"

"We do not have government systems here. There is no need. There are no wars, no fighting, no need for power. Everyone here lives under one authority. They would not even be here as a part of this kingdom if they did not all genuinely want to live in harmony and peace. Each Caprician stives to put each other on the same level as themselves. Without greed, envy, jealousy, laziness, disease, poverty, or any of that, there is not much need for a governing body beyond the scope of the guidelines set out as necessary to live here."

"Well, it seems like the perfect system without a doubt. Everyone seems so happy. But of course, I would be as well living here with all my needs met, this abundance of amazing food available at any time, clean water, air, friendly animals, such genuinely kind people, beautiful houses and the entire place looks like a gorgeous botanical garden of some sort. No longer than I have been here, I feel better than I ever have in my life." She paused for a moment, closed her eyes, and just enjoyed being completely pain free throughout her body, mind, or soul.

"My entire view of life and living has changed just in the time I have been here, even in this short amount of time, or on second thought, however long it has been." She looked at Allion to see if He might clarify that, but He made no offer to do so, so she continued, "I often spend 40, 50 or even 60 hours a week working my job. I do so primarily because I am trying to make a small difference in the lives of the kids. I also try to earn enough money to get by, pay my bills and hopefully once a year have enough extra cash to take a small trip. It is amazing to me how different things are between here and there. Before I could not have even imagined living in a world where everyone's needs were met, where everyone has plenty to eat, a nice house to live in, friends, hobbies, animals that are actually friends, where anytime they want the people can go on trips and visit all the incredible places anywhere in the world. They have all the power they need, from the water wheel and a few solar panels I saw, as well as the cleanest, freshest, healthiest water and air imaginable. Everyone here in Caprice has all of that, right?"

Allion nodded so she continued far more for herself than Allion. She just wanted to reiterate aloud how incredible this place was.

"There is no threat of war, famine, disease, or violence. I work myself to death, as do most of the people I know, day in and day out, week after week month after month, even year after year, in most cases just to stay afloat. If we are lucky, we might be able to get away for a week or two sometime, each year where we can go away from home, eat tasty food, relax, and just get away from it all. Basically, most of us are pretending we live in a world more like Caprice but just do not know it. To spend every day in a place like this with no worries, no fear, no work, other than spending a little bit of time each week contributing to the community in some way that we love and enjoy, then spend the rest of our time truly living life is amazing. It truly does feel like a fantasy. If this were not all so real, I would still believe it was some sort of hallucination, dream, or something."

"I promise you it is not a dream or hallucination. It is all very real. In fact, it is even more real than the world you came from. Your world, at least in its current state, is only temporary."

Jessie nodded her head in a statement of understanding. "I think we are all starting to realize there that it cannot withstand much more and will eventually fall if it keeps going the way it is."

"Its current state was always temporary. It was always only going to last this way for a short amount of time. I will agree with you that humans themselves cannot put a stop to it at this point. It will take an act of God to really fix the earth, unless humankind was wiped off it in one fail swoop, and that is not what God wants to do. Even after all the stuff happening there, He does still love each and every one living there. But you are right, it cannot continue the way it is."

"So, are you saying is that humanity is doomed in my world?"

"No, completely the contrary. God was always going to step in and turn things around at the predestined time. That time is remarkably close. Many of the sacred texts in your world speak of the promise of God not allowing humans to completely destroy the earth. They foretell that He will step in before that can happen and save humanity from itself."

"Well, He needs to hurry, because we are getting closer every day to a point of no return. There are many well educated and respected experts in my world that keep talking about us being closer every minute. They say we are at the tipping point of a climate disaster of such magnitude there would be no way to come back from it. It would mean the end of life on earth as we know it."

"Just keep in mind that God created the earth, so He absolutely has the power to fix it. That I can promise you. It is in His purpose to use this as a final teaching experience to show humankind that without God and His help, humanity could not survive. But with God, there will be a new heaven and a new earth."

"I have heard people talking about the new heaven all my life, but never really heard others talking about the new earth until later in life, then only a little bit here and there. I often wondered about some of the scriptures I read back in school, and afterwards in my own studies. They talked about the new heaven and new earth that you mentioned and how some of God's people would reside within both. Some of my favorite scriptures, like Matthew 5:5, even directly says, 'Blessed are the meek, for they shall inherit this new earth'. Another favorite is Psalms 37:11 and it says that as well but adds that they will also delight themselves in an abundance of peace. Yet not very many people I knew were talking about it. I am still not sure what all that means but it sure sounds an awfully lot like this place here."

Jessie thought for a little while and then said, "I remember another one of my absolute favorite scriptures about the new earth, if you would like to hear it."

"I would love to hear it." Allion smiled at her.

"It is from Isaiah Chapter 11 verses 6-9. If I remember it correctly, it says 'The wolf also shall dwell with the lamb, and the leopard shall lie down with the kid; and the calf and the young lion and the fatling together; and a little child shall lead them.

And the cow and the bear shall feed; their young ones shall lie down together: and the lion shall eat straw like the ox.

And the sucking child shall play on the hole of the asp, and the weaned child shall put his hand on the cockatrice's den.

They shall not hurt nor destroy in all my holy mountain: for the earth shall be full of the knowledge of the Lord, as the waters cover the sea. "

"Oh, I really do like that one too." Allion said as He smiled at Jessie. He looked as if He was trying to read her inner most thoughts about that scripture.

"That scripture seems to be alive and well here in Caprice."

"We are certainly living in a different stage of life here in Caprice for sure."

"So, why have I been brought here to see all of this, especially at this time, knowing that my world is so far removed from it all?"

"Because you were one of the few people that was actually listening when I called out to you."

## CARRYING THE MESSAGE

"Okay, but what am I supposed to do with this information?"

"What would you like to do with it?"

"I have no idea because in all honesty, I would rather just stay right here in Caprice for the rest of my life and not ever have to go back to my old world. This is absolutely my best fantasy of what heaven or paradise, or better yet, that new earth would look and feel like."

"What would you do if you were given the opportunity to share the hope of this world becoming a reality in your world? Is that something you would enjoy doing? Would you want to be a part of spreading that information and how it could be achieved?"

"Honestly, I am not that kind of person. I do not have any sort of platform where I could get information like that out to the public. I do not even know if the few people who are in my close network would listen to me about anything like this. I am not a minister or even a church goer for that matter."

"So, the people that know you, do they think you believe in God or heaven or a new earth or any of the things we have talked about here?"

"They all know I believe in God, the ones closest to me at least, but beyond the simplest comment occasionally, none of them know what I believe in any detail. Most days I am not even sure what I believe beyond the basics, well at least until coming here."

"If you were going to tell others about your experience here, and why you came here, what would you say or how would you start to tell them about Caprice?"

"As I have said before, I really do not even know exactly how I got here, and I did not have any sort of plan to come here. I did not even know it existed or that a place like this was possible."

"Are you sure about that?"

Jessie thought for only a moment and then went on somewhat of a rant that seemed to have been building up for a while. "I have always believed that God initially created the earth to be a beautiful worldwide garden where humans and animals could co-exist and all live happily ever after. However, it all gets a bit hazy after that as far as the destiny of the earth goes at least. There are so many contradictions between all the different religions of the world. Even within the country where I live, there are immense disagreements, even among people who all claim to be of the same Christian faith for example, not to mention all the other non-Christian belief systems. The lines seem to blur even further when they start talking about making money or having power or in recent years even about supporting one political candidate over another. It just does not make sense." She paused long enough to take a deep breath and recompose her thoughts.

"Anyway, I have always thought some sort of new earth was possible, maybe all these other religions do too in some way. However, with all that happening everywhere with so many different belief systems, seemingly at war with each other, I would have no idea how to get people to cross those lines and even envision a world where we all could all live together in harmony."

Jessie paused again and watched as the sun once again set behind the horizon and then slowly came up behind them. "It is all just so complicated. For instance, I would think that, especially any group that says they follow Jesus, would be more kind, compassionate, caring of others, going out to try to carry the message of God's love to the world, rather than just talking amongst themselves and trying to elevate their own members. I mean Jesus did say that we should follow His example and that is what He did. He traveled all around and talked to everyone, regardless of who they were."

Jessie smiled and thought to herself how much Jesus would love this place. After a moment, her thoughts went back to the religious organizations and those who were supposed to be sharing God's message. "I am sure not all, but most of the churches I know seem far more concerned with what is happening within their own walls or how much money they are bringing in than what is happening down the street or around the world. There are a lot of churches that seem to prioritize bringing in more money as their primary agenda. Jesus, who we are supposed to be following, did not appreciate that sort of exchange of money within the churches of His day. I am not saying they should not bring in some money to keep them running effectively, but it should not be their primary concern."

Jessie paused and recomposed herself and then continued, "I know it sounds like I really dislike churches. That is not really the case though, I have always enjoyed going to church. I love the singing, praising, and worshipping as well as some of the in-depth bible studies. I just always felt like it should be a lot more about getting to know God and praising Him than about money or prestige or all agreeing on some political movement, etc. It used to be a lot easier to find a nice church to attend than it is in my world today, especially with all the political chaos going on, all of which I feel has no place in church. I know it even says in our bible that as followers of Christ, we should separate ourselves from those kinds of worldly things around us, not jump in with both feet and bring them into the church itself. I know there are some religions and some churches that are not like that, but the majority in my experience are, at least in the last few years."

"I can understand why you feel that way. So, how do you think your visit here has changed your own relationship with the God of your understanding? How has it changed your view of God in general?"

Jessie thought about that for a few moments, interrupted only by the realization that somewhere along the way, Sarah had shown up with some more lemonade, as evidenced by the fact that she herself was now holding a full glass of it. She looked around but did not see Sarah anywhere in sight. So, she took a sip and continued. "As I mentioned before, I have spent a lot of time out in nature, talking and praying to God as well as reading the scriptures over and over during the past forty or so years. I just know it is very important to me to have a personal relationship with God rather than a religious one. So, I think coming here was a very natural progression to that belief, if that makes sense."

"I love how you said personal rather than religious relationship. I can certainly appreciate that desire. God surely wants a personal relationship and has always strived for that. All the individual religions of your world, as we said before, were created, set up and organized by humankind, not by God. Had God created any one of them specifically, it would have absolutely been named in those scriptures you keep referring to and it would have been explained in depth without need for so many different human interpretations all around the world. They do all play a role and do bring information about God and creation and all of it to people that would have otherwise never known about it. So, while they are not all bad, they do all veer off from the path in one way or another, especially when they cannot put down their different beliefs and work together to spread the love of God and help people be more prepared for what is about to take place."

They both sat and watched a few more sunrises and sunsets before Allion continued. "Only God knows all the ins and outs of how everything is and is supposed to be. It will, however, all be brought about in the right time and according to God's will, even in your world as it is here in

Caprice, but no one there knows the exact time, but looking around at all the things going on, the more discerning among your world, will see it getting close, just as was foretold would happen."

Jessie thought about all of that for a moment, or a few days as it was hard to tell at this point. Then she turned toward Allion and tried to look him straight in the eyes just as she realized for the first time how difficult that was. She had seen His eyes in passing and loved their beautiful ice blue with a hint of gray color. They were surrounded by beautiful laugh lines that showed years of happiness. She loved how His whole face light up when He smiled, and His eyes seemed to glisten. She had never seen anyone with eyes quite that color before either. As she thought about it, she realized she had never actually made direct eye to eye contact with Him before either. She felt so comfortable, warm, and safe around Allion but also felt an overwhelming, overpowering sense of pure magnificence, especially when she looked at Him. She supposed that knowing He was the God in this world is part of what made it difficult to look straight at Him, even in this humanoid form that He took here in Caprice.

Seeming to realize what she was thinking, Allion looked at Jessie and said, "Would you care to share what you are thinking?"

Nervously Jessie changed her thoughts back to what they had been talking about before she tried to look directly at Him. "So, as the God and Creator of Caprice, I bet you know a lot about, well everything in the world and all existence, including my own world huh?"

"Yes, Jessie I do. In fact, if you seek, you will find, that I AM. I am everywhere."

"Wait, what are you saying? I am not sure I understand what you mean when you say that."

Allion placed His hand very lovingly on Jessie's shoulder and gently said, "I am the Alpha and Omega, the Beginning and the End, the First and the Last, the ONE True God and Creator." Then He turned and sat back in His seat and looked out over the horizon to give Jessie time to comprehend what He had just told her.

As a shock wave went through her entire being, Jessie simultaneously felt a complete sense of awe and an immediate understanding that this Allion, whom she had spent all this time with here in Caprice, was the God of her world as well. She now knew He was the only God and creator of everything in existence. It took a while for her brain to process that information. She just sat silently for several more rotations of the sun, as it seemed to continue to circle where they were sitting. She was not sure she could have spoken even if she had wanted to do so. She had no idea what to say in response to this new information.

Then suddenly for the first time since arriving in Caprice, the passing of time seemed to come to a complete standstill.

Nothing moved at all. The only thing she could even hear were her own thoughts. It might have been seconds, or hours or days even. Then suddenly she felt Allion put His arm around her shoulders. She immediately felt all the weight she had ever carried lifted from her. The next thing she knew she was crying again much like she did that first night underneath the gorgeous Caprician sky. She was again releasing all pain, worry, frustration, fear, and anything else of that nature she had ever carried within her throughout her entire life. Immediately following that emotional explosion, she felt the greatest sense of peace and comfort that she had ever known in her life.

Once she was finally able to speak again, Jessie said, "So, I am a bit confused, about a lot of things but let's start with your name. I had never heard the name Allion before coming here. I have heard many different names for God in my world, like Yahweh, Jehovah, Allah, I AM, Elohim and many others. I am sure there are a lot of them I do not know around the world. We have over one hundred of them just in our bible, but Allion is not one of any that I have ever heard even mentioned. So, what is the deal with that name? Are you in fact, the same God as the one that created the world where I live?"

"You are right. I am known by hundreds of names just in your own world. I am also known by many different names around the world here in

Caprice. But there is only one true God and Creator and I just happen to be Him." He winked at Jessie and continued. "All of creation knows me by the name they have been taught or somehow learned from someone before them. Even in Heaven, I am called a few different names at various times and for different reasons. Allion is just quite a common one here in Caprice, especially among young children. They love it so much. They have even made up some very lovely songs about it." He looked down toward the field far below them, as the sounds of children's laughter floated up to them on the breeze. "I sure do love that sound."

He looked back at Jessie and smiled as He continued, "I assure you, I am that God, your creator, your father, your mother, as I said, I am the Great I AM." He paused only for a moment and then continued, "Not to throw another wrench in all of this for you, but I also appear in many forms to different people as well, even here in Caprice. They do not all see me the same way you do. To you, I am a loving, kind, gentle, soft-spoken grandfather. To some, I am a grandmother, to others, a small child and playmate. It all depends on the person, the time, and their need. I am all things to those in need."

Jessie spoke softly and said, "How can my mind be completely blown and so at peace at the same time?" They both just smiled and watched another sunset and sunrise as time once again picked back up to full speed.

The next thing she knew she saw Sarah walking up the hill with more of that lemonade she loved so much. It felt like months since she had that last glass that appeared out of nowhere, so she was quite excited to see her bringing them some.

"Hi Jessie. I thought you might be ready for something to drink."

"Yes, Thank you." She turned to look at Allion, half expecting Him to be gone like He often was when someone else appeared, but He was still there and took a glass of lemonade for Himself as well.

He winked at Jessie and said, "Not taking off this time before I have myself some of this delicious lemonade." He looked at Sarah and smiled, then they all three laughed. Jessie took a huge drink of hers and looked down at her glass to realize it was still completely full. She laughed, looked up at Sarah then back at Allion, but this time He was gone.

Sarah sat down beside Jessie and looked out over the mountain ranges. They sat there quietly for a few minutes then Sarah said, "It sounds like you have some big decisions to make. How are you feeling about that?"

"What decisions? What do you mean?"

"This knowledge that you have been given while here in Caprice about how God intended your world to be and how it can be achieved. What are you going to do with it?"

"I don't know anything I can do with it. I mean I explained to Allion, who told me who He is, that I don't have any sort of platform to get this information out to the people in my world. I just don't. I mean I have a very small bubble of people around me. I don't really do social media. I don't even go to church and am not a part of any big organization of any sort. I really do not have the means to share this information with anyone really. Come to think of it, I should have suggested that He bring Cody here next time. She is much more outgoing than I am, and it was her house after all, where all this took place.

"Well, you know what Allion would say to that?"

"Something philosophical, I am sure."

They both laughed and then Sarah continued, "He would say that He does not call the qualified, but rather qualifies the ones whom He calls and that are listening."

"He basically said the exact same thing earlier to me."

"Did he tell you the whole Moses story about him having a speech impediment but that he was still the chosen one to bring the ten commandments to the world?"

"No, He did not tell me that part. But I have heard the story. I just really do not see where I have anything it takes to help the world head back in the right direction."

Jessie thought back to the comment Allion made earlier about her listening and thought that had something to do with it all.

"I know you do not think you have the means to get this word out there or effect any change in your world yourself. But you are so far ahead of a lot of people in your world. You have worked years to develop such a close personal relationship with Him. Then you opened your heart, mind, and soul enough to hear whatever messages of hope He sent your way. You listened to Him call you forward. Then you trusted in Him and in yourself enough to walk through that door into Caprice. You have a positive attitude. You are quite resilient and determined to go through each of the necessary processes to find out where it takes you. THAT is what landed you here and that is ALL you need to take you where you need to go. That is why you are so important to this call, to this mission, to your world. I know all of that for a fact, because you are still sitting right here going through this part of the process."

They both sat for what seemed like only a few seconds, but in other ways, it felt like several days.

Then Sarah continued, "The only pieces of the puzzle you were missing before included the information and clarification of God's intention as well as how it could absolutely all work together. You have those now and with God and His angels on your side, there is no way you could fail, whether it is one person you need to reach or millions. You have everything it takes to do your part in helping to fulfill God's purpose. We all do. We have all been called for different things and each one of us has a purpose to fulfill. You, like everyone else, have already fulfilled some of your purposes, and now you have been called directly to fulfill another one. But the choice is absolutely yours. What will you do?"

"Well, when you put it that way, what else can I do? I guess I must give it a try. But I do not even know where to begin." She felt tears streaming down her face at the gut-wrenching thought of leaving Caprice and going back to her own treacherous world.

Now it was Sarah's turn to put her arm around Jessie's shoulders. "I will make you a promise. In fact, God has already made this promise to everyone."

Jessie looked up at her in desperation. "I promise God's Kingdom will be waiting for you and as His Son once said, I will be there with you in paradise."

Jessie expected another emotional outburst at any moment to rise from her very core, but something different was happening. She was starting to feel a peace like she had never known, not even here in Caprice. She felt hope, understanding, confidence and an assuredness of God's promises to be fulfilled, that would have been beyond her comprehension just a little while ago.

"It's a good feeling, isn't it?"

"Yes. Yes, it is."

"I really do not understand though, how I can spread this knowledge of God's will for the earth or tell people how to achieve it. I mean Caprice is incredible but there is no way my world could just suddenly change to be more like this place. The way of life there pretty much revolves 100% around money, politics, religious opposition, and just surviving from one day to the next in most cases. I would not have a clue how to tell even one person all that I have learned here. I do not even totally understand it myself and certainly have no clue how this place came into being."

"I have one small bit of information you might need to move forward. You do not have to have all the answers. Think about the people that God has called to do different things in your world, even in the scriptures. He called many different people and each one with a slightly different message or calling. Your calling is only to plant the seed and get others to look to God for the answers to the world's problems. You do not have to tell each one how to achieve every aspect of it in their lives. However, you do have the necessary knowledge behind you now to share enough understanding with the world to give them hope of another way of living life, of God's way of living. God will send the right people in your direction and send you in the right direction of the people He needs you to reach.

All that is asked of you is to be willing to share what you have learned here and begin to put as many of these things into practice in your own life as possible. By doing these two things, you will encourage others to see the world with a bit more hope and understanding from this point forward."

"Well, that does make more sense than anything else right now. I suppose it is all about a leap of faith at this point."

"It absolutely is. Sometimes you just take that first step and then the next one and then the next one. It is all about the journey and the perpetual forward movement. It will all happen as it needs to, and the right people will all come along and share the journey with you and you them. Just like here in Caprice. None of us could complete this world without the others, well except for Allion of course."

"Of course." They both smiled at each other.

After a moment Jessie said, "Well there is a bit of a movement going on in my world where quite a few people are becoming interested in more sustainable practices. They are growing some of their own food or at least learning how to do so. Many are also trying to find other ways to take care of themselves and their families if it all goes crumbling down to the ground one day. I never really thought much about it before, until now of course, but it makes a lot of sense that God could just step in at any time and hit the stop button."

Sarah nodded in agreement that it could happen but then said, "Maybe He has called enough people and given them the right pieces of the puzzle to start heading earth back in the right direction before all of that happens. That is how He does things."

"Come to think of it, that is true and even more likely. Who would have ever guessed any of this? I know I would not have done so if I had not seen it with my own eyes and personally lived it for, well however long I have been here." Jessie said as she looked at Sarah hoping for some clue as to how long she had been in Caprice.

Sarah just smiled and said, "It sounds like you have made your decision. Just always check your motives with each step and action forward. Remember all you saw here and how incredible God's Kingdom can be. Do that and you will accomplish exactly what you are supposed to do."

"Yes, it sounds like that to me too. But I can tell you one thing, I am not going anywhere without another piece of that pumpkin pie of yours!"

They both burst out laughing, got up from the bench and headed back toward Sarah's cabin.

As they went along, Charlie stepped out of the woods, came over to the path and walked so close to Jessie that his fur brushed up against her hand. She automatically and without any residual hesitation began to pet his fur. He obviously loved every second of it. After a couple of minutes, he suddenly stopped in his tracks. Jessie stopped and looked back at him. The glimmer in his eye and demeanor of his whole body told her all she needed to know about what he was thinking. He then sat down on the ground and lifted a paw in her direction. "I will also be here waiting for you. Hurry home and remember, we are all on this same journey together, whether we know it or not. We might as well all go together."

She felt more than heard that statement from Charlie, then nodded in agreement.

A moment later it seemed, they were sitting on Sarah's porch having a huge piece of pie, along with a nice cup of coffee loaded with Jessie's new favorite cashew milk creamer and laughing about all the things that had occurred since Jessie first arrived, especially that first morning when Charlie scared her so bad outside the bedroom window.

"So many things are just not as they first appear to be." Sarah said.

"I definitely understand that better than ever before."

"Never forget that for a moment." Said a familiar voice behind her as she turned to see Allion walking out the door of the cabin with His own plate of pie.

"How can I still be startled when He does that?" Jessie said and they all broke out laughing with Jessie.

"I have to say that was the best piece of pie yet. You have really outdone yourself once again. Thank you as well for your hospitality while I have been here."

"It has been our pleasure. As we said to start with, we are all so very glad you decided to visit and stay with us for a bit."

"I cannot take it any longer. I want to know how long I have been here. I still cannot figure out this time thing and how it works here."

Allion and Sarah glanced at each other with a smile and then Sarah said, "That is because time does not exist here. As Allion would say, a day is as a thousand years and a thousand years as a day. You have been here for many rotations of the sun, but it feels as though you have only been here a few minutes to me. I wish it could be longer. But I know, I will see you again soon."

"We will all see you again," several additional voices rang out at once around her. Dani with an

I, Greg, Gracie, Katie, and several others were all there, as if to wish her goodbye.

At that moment, Gracie came running over to Jessie and said before you go, you must see the butterfly tree with me! Please."

"Okay, Okay. I would love to." Gracie grabbed Jessie by the hand and gently pulled her across the lawn. Jessie looked back and waved to everyone. They all waved back with such love and kindness. She was still overwhelmed with gratitude and happiness just being here and meeting all these Capricians."

As they rounded the corner of trees to the right of the meadow, Gracie called out, "It is right up here. You are going to love it."

"Oh, I am sure I will. I love butterflies."

A moment later they were lying on the ground next to each other, looking up at the sky, watching thousands of butterflies of all different kinds fluttering about in the most surreal and incredible display Jessie had ever seen. Millions of colors it seemed, all moving together in an astonishing dance of wings just above her. Jessie closed her eyes and could feel the butterflies lightly tickling her skin as they softly landed all over her.

"Isn't this amazing?" She heard Gracie say, but she was so mesmerized she could not bring herself to respond. "This is one of my favorite things about Caprice. How about you?" Gracie asked, but Jessie was still unable to speak, she was so caught up in the moment.

"Jessie, did you hear me? Earth calling Jessie, come in Jessie."

She slowly realized that was a different but completely familiar voice. She slowly opened her eyes.

"Jessie. Are you in there Jessie?" Cody laughed as she nudged Jessie in the side. "We are about ready to eat, and you have been starting at that picture long enough."

Jessie turned her head slightly to the left and saw Cody standing there next to her, smiling from ear to ear.

Jessie laughed then hugged her and said, "Yes, I am ready to eat. Thank you for inviting me here today."

"Oh my gosh, I would not have it any other way. I am so glad to hear you say that. Now come on, let's eat."

They both walked down the hallway toward the dining room. As they reached the door, Jessie saw the room was full of people standing around talking and laughing. They were all holding plates in their hands and looked ready to dive into the multitude of dishes sitting on the long table in the middle of the room.

Cody spoke up and asked Dave, another cousin of theirs, if he would be so kind as to say a prayer before the meal.

"I would be honored."

As he began to pray, everyone bowed their head and closed their eyes, including Jessie. However, as she did, she felt Allion standing right next to her. A feeling of joy she could not express came over her, knowing she would never feel too far from God ever again.

Dave began speaking.

"Dear Jehovah God,

Thank you for all this food we have laid out here before us and please bless the hands that have prepared it. We are grateful for every single person who is here with us today and most of all for your presence in our lives. We ask these things and give thanks in the name of your Son Jesus. Amen."

"Amen" was heard around the room and then a rush of chatter from everyone. Spoons and such were clattering, and the oohs and ahs were coming from all directions.

Jessie grabbed a plate and dug in as well. Just as she reached the end of the table and finished loading her dish with at least a dozen various kinds of vegetables, she heard another familiar voice.

"Jessie. Would you care to sit with us?"

She looked around to see two older women sitting at a dressed-up card table with plates as full as hers. One of them was the lady she met when she first arrived at the reunion, the one who made the lemonade. Jessie smiled and headed over to where they were. A new warmth rose inside of her that she had never felt in a group like this before today, at least not this side of Caprice.

As she approached the table, the lady said, "I am not sure if I properly introduced myself before, but my name is Lucinda, and this is Cara. Cara, this is Jessie McCallin. I remember her when she was a little kid. She was always such a bright child. She was one of my students when I first started teaching and of course she was always a favorite."

"Nice to meet you, Jessie." Cara said.

Before Jessie could reply, Lucinda turned to look at Jessie and said, "I have heard you now do an impressive service helping kids in need. We are all so proud to have you in our family."

Jessie was just as shocked by that statement as she was about anything else that had happened in the past, well however long it had been since she walked through Cody's front door. She glanced up at the clock on the wall across from her and realized it had only been about 45 minutes ago. She felt a smile come across her face and she genuinely said, "It is so nice to meet you both." She pulled out her chair and sat down.

The next hour or so was a rush of conversations about different people both known to be at the reunion and those they had not seen yet. Jessie had no idea who most of them were, but Lucinda and Cara knew them all, at least as intimately as they did her anyway. Jessie smiled and joined in where she could and truly did enjoy her meal with them.

As they finished their meal and began the formalities of cleaning up after themselves and saying their goodbyes, Jessie turned her attention to finding Cody. That task did not take long in the end as she was just out on the front porch enjoying a last bite of cake.

Jessie walked over to her and said, "What a wonderful party and such a gorgeous place for it. Thank you for having us all here."

Cody nodded and smiled so genuinely that Jessie felt it all through her being. "It is definitely my pleasure all the way around."

Jessie then leaned over close to her and said, "Were you serious about me hanging out for a day or two and maybe help clean up after the party?"

"I was absolutely serious about you hanging out. Oh, I would be so delighted. Please say you will."

"I would love nothing more! I do need to just pop home and grab a couple of things though and water my plants."

"Please do come back. That would be the cherry on the top of the entire party for me."

Jessie hugged her and said, "You got it. I promise."

Jessie made her way down the steps and back across the beautiful lawn. The crisp, fresh, autumn air and the stunning array of fall colors all around her was breathtaking. She felt like a completely different person than she was just upon arriving earlier that day. She was a completely different person right down to her very soul. She also had a new mission in life, with no idea how to carry it out. However, she was sure with God's and Cody's help, she could figure out a way to begin it.

Later that evening, Jessie and Cody sat on the back porch and watched the sun go down over the mountains as they had a nice warm cup of cocoa. Jessie could not believe how beautiful the sunset was as it set behind the blue mountains in the distance. It might not have been as extraordinary as those she saw in Caprice, but it was one of the most beautiful sunsets she had seen this side of it.

"I really do love your new house, Cody. I love the land too and that you have more room here than at your old place. Are you still going to plant a garden here?"

"Oh, without a doubt. I have enough room for a nice greenhouse too! I cannot wait. I have always wanted one of my own."

"I think that is a splendid idea!"

They watched the sky for a couple more minutes and then Jessie continued. "I have actually been thinking about getting a little place of my own as well, some place with a yard and room for a small garden, maybe even stick up a solar panel or two."

"Oh wow. That is amazing. I love that idea. But I am curious. What brought that on?" Cody asked a bit surprised because Jessie loved her apartment. She loved it so much it was hard to get out of it for any amount of time at all.

"I want to share something with you. You are the only person on earth that might not think I have lost my mind. You most likely will anyway, but I still would like to share it with you, if that is okay?"

"Of course, you can always share anything with me. Besides, I already think you are a little crazy. We all are a little bit from time to time. How boring would life be if we weren't? So go on, give it your best shot."

Jessie slowly began to fill Cody in on her journey to Caprice. As she did so, Jessie carefully watched Cody's expressions to see if she could tell at which moment she thought she had gone over the edge. However, Cody just listened and took it all in as if listening to a beautiful song. The musical background was a chorus of frogs and crickets as Cody's backyard became increasingly alive and darkness began to fall. The more she talked about it all, the faster she went and by the end she was so excited that could barely contain herself or her excitement.

When she reached the end of her story, she looked out over the lawn to wait for Cody's reply.

"What an incredible experience. Wow. I cannot imagine having an opportunity to visit such a place as God's Kingdom. I have dreamed of what it must be like so many times. However, to experience it in whatever way you just did, had to be one of those once in a lifetime experiences." Cody thought for a second and then said, "Well obviously for you, a twice in a lifetime experience." I am so happy for you! Seeing how excited you are about it all and about God as well as all that might entail moving forward really makes me happy too."

"Thank you. I am just so glad you don't think I have lost it."

"Not at all. I have had moments of my own, where I knew without a doubt that God was there talking to me. I mean I could absolutely feel Him standing there with me. Although I never actually got to visit His kingdom before, this kind of validates my own ideas about it all."

"Wow. I knew I could talk to you about it but did not expect you to take it this well."

"They both laughed and sat staring toward the distant mountain range as fireflies starting to light up here and there around the yard."

"I have no idea on earth how I could ever get this message out to the people that are supposed to hear it. I just do not have that kind of reach. You are, at least until now, my entire social circle. On second thought, maybe this is mission accomplished." They both laughed.

"Let's put our heads together and figure this out. I do know enough about this kind of stuff to know, that if God is giving you that little voice inside, it will not stop until you do it. We have got this, lets figure it out."

Jessie quietly whispered, "God, help us. In Jesus' name. Amen."

Cody quietly whispered, "Amen."

They both sat there for quite some time and suddenly Cody spoke up. "I have the perfect plan.

"Let's hear it."

"You could write a book! I can help. We can do this together!"

"For real, you would help me do that?" Jessie asked excitedly, then continued before Cody could answer. "I agree, that is kind of the perfect plan, and I would love to do it with you!"

"Absolutely, none of us can do it all on our own. But working together, with God's help, we have got this!"

Invitation to Share the Journey

For anyone who would like more information about Caprice or the promises that have been made concerning the new earth, in the holy scriptures and many other texts throughout history, please feel free to check out our website.

www.CapriceGardens.com

Now that this book is complete, we will begin adding all the references and resources used to complete this writing there.

We will also continue to add information on how individuals can experience their own version of Caprice or move in that direction one step at a time.

Self (or as we call it) God Sustainability is not nearly as hard or complicated as most people believe. Come join us and share the journey and we will help each other along the way.

Made in United States
Orlando, FL
17 April 2024